Tease Me Not

Madeleine Rosa

Contents

Chapter 1

itty Alcott giggled uncontrollably as she and her closest friend, Evangeline Dawson, escaped the clutches of the elderly Sir Walter Martin. They hid behind a pillar in the ballroom of her home at Ethridge laughing.

"Did you see the way he looked at you?" Evangeline panted. "Such lust, it was so hilarious! You are such a tease, Kitty!" She clutched the sides of her thin waist with her arms.

Kitty rolled her eyes laughing. "Don't I know it, Eva? I don't care, it was so much fun!"

"If you had flirted with him any longer I would bet my dowry that you would have had an offer from him by the end of the night!" Evangeline exclaimed amidst her giggles.

Kitty scoffed. "Then I would reject it, like I do with the rest of the offers turned my way."

Kitty enjoyed playing with people. She knew it was wrong but London society was boring, without her playfulness she would not be able to bear it. She had found a companion in Evangeline. Evangeline enjoyed playing and laughing as much as Kitty did. Kitty used her beauty to her advantage. She had deep brown hair that twisted in perfect ringlets and mysterious, dark blue eyes. She was of average height and had a very lovely figure that men found irresistible.

"What is your father going to say when he finds out about Sir Walter?" Evangeline asked once she could control her laughter.

Kitty smirked at her best friend. "My papa could never be angry at me. He'll just find out that Sir Walter was pining after me and then want to shoot him. I'll be the innocent victim in all of this."

Evangeline grinned devilishly. "You are devious, aren't you?"

"Of course, how is one to have any fun in this town if they're not?" Kitty giggled. "I could not bear a London season if I wasn't, you know. All these society men are a frightful bore; if I did not have some fun then I would declare myself a spinster and happily move to my grandmamma's farm in Yorkshire."

Evangeline's expression suddenly turned serious. "Have you ever ... spent the night with a man?" she whispered.

Kitty gasped in horror. "Darling, I'm spirited not stupid!"

"Good, that would be stupid," Evangeline breathed a sigh of relief. Evangeline was also one of the beauties in the ton. She had lovely golden hair and tantalizing hazel eyes that enticed suitors into her midst. She turned her head back towards the ballroom and sighed. "Shall we go find another few partners, how is your dance card looking?"

Kitty smiled gleefully. "I never have any space, I walk into a room and it is filled within minutes. The annoying this is that mama and papa are wondering why I have not selected a husband. It is my third season after all and I am one and twenty."

Her parents were truly wonderful, and she loved them for it, but she wished they would not keep bothering her about marriage. Kitty was a good sister though, her younger sister Little J was breaking the rules most frightfully every day and she never gave her up. She wasn't seeing a man or anything; she was just embracing her gift, the gift of intelligence. As Kitty didn't have any other gift than beauty, she used it to her advantage. She didn't want to get married, at least not yet. Once she was married it meant she was bound to one man's arm for the rest of her days. She was having far too much fun being a debutante then she would if she was a wife.

Evangeline rolled her eyes. "It is the same with my parents," she groaned. "I never get any peace. Papa has invited a guest to stay with us for a few weeks in the hopes that a courtship might blossom."

Kitty's jaw dropped. "You never said a word! Who is this man?" she asked, intrigued.

Evangeline shrugged her shoulders. "I've not a clue," she said disinterestedly. "He's titled, I believe, I think a young baronet who's just inherited."

Kitty giggled. "A young baronet?" she raised her eyebrows. "Who knows, perhaps he might be handsome enough to tempt the beautiful Lady Evangeline Dawson."

Evangeline scoffed. "I doubt it," she nudged her friend. "I would rather die a spinster than move from town. I'm not about to retire to some frightfully boring estate in the middle of nowhere just for a title."

"Bravo," Kitty commended. "I'm proud of you, my dear. Now, let's go back inside before anyone notices our absence."

The two young ladies walked arm in arm back into the ballroom which was filled with unmarried ladies and gentleman, not to mention their parents who were all anxiously watching the acquaintances their children were making.

Kitty spotted her cousin dancing timidly with one of the military men that were in town for the season. She always felt sorry for poor Sabine. Her Aunt Jane and Uncle Daniel always shipped her off to London for the season even though Sabine hated it. Sabine and Kitty were complete opposites. Sabine loved horses and literature and Kitty loved balls and dancing. Even though they had nothing in common Kitty felt as though Sabine was her third sister and a dear friend. Sabine often spent the time in town trying to control Kitty, without much success.

The ballroom was awfully abundant with bluecoats that evening. Her father had invited practically the entire navy to attend the ball which she found most amusing considering how against his daughters marrying militiamen he was.

Kitty tended to steer clear of the military men. They were nice enough company if one wanted to soil her reputation.

The Royal Navy was stationed in and around London for the summer, with their grand ships docked nearby.

Almost as soon as they two women entered the ballroom, Evangeline was claimed by her quadrille partner and was whisked off to dance. Kitty's quadrille partner was a man named Sir Harold Croft and Kitty felt as if she had to accept his invitation since it was rude to refuse. She decided to try and escape him by making her way into the crowds of people.

By doing so she inadvertently ran into her parents who were standing talking to a naval officer with her twin brother, James. She was glad that she and James looked nothing alike as they had grown. They shared the same blue eye colour and brown hair colour but they were completely different in every way which she was thankful for. She loved her brother, as any sister should, but he was a womaniser. He enjoyed many women, and he was being punished for it. For the remainder of the season he was not allowed to leave their parents side of risk being cut off financially.

"Kitty," her mother exclaimed, surprised. "I am surprised you have no partner for the quadrille, it is your favourite dance!"

Kitty smiled at her mother and stood beside her. "Alas, I don't, but no matter, it is nice to have a break every now and then. One can tire so easily from dancing all night." It was then that she decided to look up to the naval officer that had been conversing with her parents. He was looking at her most curiously, as most men did when they first saw the famous Lady Kitty Alcott.

But even Kitty had to admit that he was handsome. His dark blond hair was quite long hand was combed back neatly for the benefit of the occasion. His eyes were a piercing, bright blue, and they almost hypnotised her. He was wearing his fancy naval uniform that emphasised his lean physique. He bowed politely to her, so she curtseyed back to him.

"Captain, this is my eldest daughter, Lady Kitty, Kitty, this is Captain William Aubrey, these are his officers," her father introduced.

Kitty was impressed. It was not often that a captain was so young. She was sure that he was a good leader.

"I've heard many things, Lady Kitty," he smiled at her, but she couldn't help but feel it was out of politeness and not want.

"Good things I hope," she smiled back warmly, attempting to begin a flirtation with him.

Captain Aubrey didn't answer her. Instead he turned back to her father. "I thank you for the invitation, Lord Ethridge, but I don't think it would be appropriate for me to stay at your residence when my men are housed elsewhere, it wouldn't give them the right impression. It would make me feel as though I was above them."

Kitty's eyes widened. She couldn't believe her father had asked a naval officer to stay with them considering how he felt about them. "But aren't you above them, Captain?" Kitty asked. "You are in charge, after all."

Captain Aubrey's eyes narrowed on Kitty. It made her feel uncomfortable that he was not charmed by her. She hadn't met a man that had not fallen for her charms. "Perhaps I am above them in military rank, Lady Kitty, but it does not mean that I am better than them."

Her mother cut in before she could reply. Kitty did not know what this man's problem was. Surely if she had an opportunity to speak with him alone she would be able to melt the ice that surrounded him. She would lose all confidence in herself if she could not. "Captain Aubrey, I know of four and twenty families who are hosting an officer, would you not consider it?"

Captain Aubrey paused for a minute before nodding. "It is a very kind offer, milady, milord," he said, thanking her parents. "I would be glad to stay for a short while."

"Excellent," her father smiled happily. "Now, why don't you enjoy the ball? Kitty, if you're unoccupied for this dance then go and show the Captain how it's done, I implore you."

Much to Kitty's dismay, Captain Aubrey seemed to be reluctant. Nevertheless, he offered Kitty his arm and she accepted it timidly. Once they were out of earshot, she began to work her charms. "Naval work must be very dangerous," she commented delicately. "I'd wager you a brave man."

Captain Aubrey frowned down at her. "It can be dangerous at times, yes," he nodded.

"I'd imagine you like being at port, there are many beautiful sights to be seen in London," she said, her voice thicker this time. She was being very obvious but the man would not relent. He seemed determined to ignore her. Did he think himself better than her? She was the eldest daughter of an Earl after all!

"I prefer the sea," he stated simply. When they reached the dancing circle he pulled his arm from her grasp and made sure there was an appropriate distance between the two of them. "I have no intention of dancing with you, now, Lady Kitty, so if you'll excuse me." With that he turned away from her and began to make his way back into the crowd.

That action infuriated her. How dare he just leave her there like some common bar wench that he'd just bedded. She would not stand for it. She picked up her skirts and marched after him, she wanted an explanation for his rude actions.

He was heading outside the ballroom where she and Evangeline had escaped previously to. 'Good' she thought, 'He'll be alone'.

She followed him out the ballroom doors and into the outside courtyard. She found him immediately looking out into the night at the cloudless sky. If she weren't so angry with him then she might've found the action quite admirable.

"Captain," she said angrily.

Captain Aubrey immediately stiffened and turned towards her. "Lady Kitty, what have I done to drag you from your kingdom?" he asked, almost cynically.

Her eyes narrowed on him. "You dare mock me?" she gasped. "Don't you know who I am?"

"I know exactly who you are, Lady Kitty, you are the eldest daughter of the Earl of Ethridge," he stated simply.

What was he playing at? "Why did you leave me there instead of dancing with me?" she demanded to know after a moment of silence.

"The dance did not belong to me, it belonged to Sir Harold Croft," he shrugged, turning away from her and letting his eyes return to the night sky.

Kitty paused. "How did you know that?" she asked, appearing quite startled.

"It is part of my job to be very astute, Lady Kitty; I am trained to notice things that many others will not. For example the first thing I noticed when I entered this ballroom was the brunette beauty on the dance floor. I learned her name from a few of my officers and then the fact that she never had a spare dance on her card from several of her jilted partners. I then learned that she makes it her business to flirt and tease every man with a penny to his name. You want to know how I knew the quadrille belonged to Sir Harold Croft? I heard him asking for you when you separated from your silly friend." He spoke without looking at her. Instead he just continued staring at the sky.

Kitty didn't know what to say. She didn't know whether to be happy that he noticed her beauty or to be insulted that he'd practically described her every action in one mono-logue. "Do you think yourself very clever, Captain Aubrey?" Kitty asked in a careful tone.

"If you count observations as intelligence, then yes," he nodded, still not looking at her.

"Are you trying to insult me, Captain Aubrey?" Kitty asked, trying to mask whatever hurt had made its way into her voice.

"It was an observation, Lady Kitty," he reiterated. He then chose to look at her and Kitty wished she did not look so vulnerable. "I make it my business to see through people. I am good at deducing their motives."

Kitty no longer thought Captain Aubrey handsome. She didn't like him one bit. He did not have her deduced. He was wrong. He could not sum her up in a matter of sentences; she was not some ridiculous flirt. "I should think you would want to practice your craft, Captain, for I fear you are terribly inaccurate," she said acidly.

"Am I?" Captain Aubrey raised his eyebrows questioningly. "If you think I need practice then I should have plenty of time to perfect it whilst I am residing her at Ethridge."

Kitty huffed impatiently before turning on her heel to head back into the ball. That Captain Aubrey was a cunning cad that she did not like one bit and she would make it her mission to make his stay at Ethridge anything but pleasant.

Chapter 2

Kitty was unable to enjoy the rest of the ball after Captain Aubrey had called her on her behaviour. She danced the rest of her dances but it felt more like obligation to her rather than for pure enjoyment.

She was happy when dawn came and the guests began to depart her house. All guests of course except for Captain William Aubrey.

As Kitty went upstairs to sleep for a few hours before breakfast she ran into Little J who was in the process of sneaking out, like she did every day. Her younger sister had so much potential to be one of the most beautiful debutantes in society but she refused to participate in such activities. She was blessed with lovely blonde hair and pretty blue eyes. "And where are going?" Kitty asked in a knowing tone.

"Out," Little J answered quickly as she hurried past her sister. Kitty noticed how she carried with her a small brown satchel that looked quite full.

"Little J," she said disapprovingly. "You're sure you're not doing anything illegal? I'm your sister, you should be able to tell me where you go off to every day," Kitty moaned.

Little J pursed her lips. "It's not illegal … I don't think," she said awkwardly. "I've told you I'm not ruining myself, and I'm using my intelligence to my advantage, what more do you want?" she sighed to her elder sister. "Kitty, don't ask questions," she pleaded. "I'll tell you soon, I promise."

Kitty frowned. "I'll hold you to that, Little J," she said seriously.

Little J smiled and quickly kissed her sister's cheek. "I love you, tell mama and papa I've gone to Annie's!" she called over her shoulder as she disappeared out of the house.

Kitty covered for Little J each day. Today's excuse was that she was going to their youngest sister's house that was about a mile away. Annie had married young to their young reverend who'd taken over the church once his father had passed away. Annie and Mr Joseph Preston had been fools for each other since childhood, and her father approved the match because of how genuine Joseph was. She was happy that her shy little sister had found someone who brought out the best in her. They'd been married about a year and her mother was anxiously awaiting the news that she was going to be a grandmother.

As soon as she'd entered her bedchamber the door opened once more and her mother entered. Kitty thought her mother had truly aged gracefully considering she was now in her mid forties. Her hair was still its lovely golden colour and her figure was the same as it had always been.

"You looked lovely this evening, my dear," she smiled.

Kitty smiled back. "Thank you, mama," she replied. "As did you."

Emilia scoffed, rolling her eyes. "I'll pretend I believe you," she laughed.

Kitty decided against entering into that discussion with her mother. Emilia would win.

"Sit with me, darling," Emilia instructed as she sat down on Kitty's bed. Kitty sat beside her mother who immediately wrapped her arms around her and kissed her forehead. Kitty enjoyed sitting with her mother, it reminded her of being a child. She'd had a good childhood. Her parents were truly one of a kind. "This is your third season," she said softly.

Kitty stiffened and pulled away from her mother. "Mama, what are you getting at?" she demanded to know.

Emilia's eyes narrowed. "Captain Aubrey is not only a highly decorated militiaman; he's also made his fortune in the navy. It was your father's idea..." she said awkwardly.

Kitty shivered at the thought. "Absolutely not," she snapped.

"What reason do you have to refuse?" Emilia demanded. "He is a gentleman, he's handsome and he's wealthy, so you know he won't want you for your dowry. I would have thought you would jump at this idea."

"Well, clearly you don't understand me, mama," Kitty said cynically. "You will not force a match there."

Emilia's eyes narrowed as she rose from the bed. "What reason have you to reject him?" she asked angrily.

Kitty could have listed ten reasons, all stemming from their cold encounter the night before but she wasn't a snitch. "Mama, Captain Aubrey does not tempt me, can you please let it go?" she sighed.

Emilia looked at Kitty sadly. "Don't you want to get married and start your own family?" she asked hopefully.

Kitty did want those things someday, but she enjoyed her seasons too much to settle. "Mama, if I promise to let you know when someone catches my eye, will you drop this?" she pleaded.

Emilia conceded defeat and nodded. "I'm only looking out for you, Kitty. I have your best interests at heart."

Kitty smiled and put her arms around her mother's neck. "I know you do, and I love you for it," she smiled.

"Not as much as I love you, my dear," she kissed her forehead once more. "Now get some sleep. We've the military salute tonight at Sir Walter Martin's residence. He's a kindly fellow, isn't he? Word was that he fancied you, did you know?" her mother informed her innocently.

Kitty rolled her eyes and groaned. "Good night, mama," she said in a dismissing tone.

"Sleep well, I'll wake you in a few hours," Emilia laughed lightly as she exited the room.

Kitty wished she'd asked a maid to assist her in undressing before she'd retired. She did her bed to unbutton her gown with little success. In the end she decided to climb into bed still wearing her ball gown. As she lay staring at the canopy above her head she couldn't believe what had happened in the past evening.

Her flirtations with Sir Walter Martin were her own fault. She'd forgotten that he was hosting the military salute the next night which meant that not only would he be receiving her and her family upon their arrival, it meant that he would be seeking her out for more dances. What made it worse was that the ball was a military salute which meant that all the blue and red coats in town would be in attendance – including the delightful Captain Aubrey.

She closed her eyes lethargically, willing sleep to clear her head.

She was awoken by her mother at ten o'clock for breakfast. As her mother helped her change, Kitty decided that she wouldn't let anything bother her for her season. She was young and lively and there was nothing wrong with that. She wasn't going to let anything that Captain Aubrey said get to her, nor was she going to fret about the men she'd charmed. She would have fun, that's what balls were for after all.

When she arrived down at breakfast her family were already seated. As she and her mother entered the room both her brothers, her father and Captain Aubrey stood. Emilia took her seat next to Sebastian and Kitty took her seat next to her mother as the eldest daughter. Sitting across from her was her brother, James, and next to him was Captain Aubrey. Her seventeen year old brother, Henry, who was home from Eton for the summer, sat next to her also.

"Kitty, where has Little J gotten to this morning?" her father asked her. "I feel as though I never see her."

Kitty knew James was aware of what Little J was up to. He always looked away or down at his hands whenever her whereabouts were mentioned. "She's gone to Annie's this morning, papa, she said she would be gone for the day," Kitty lied smoothly.

Sebastian frowned. "Did she at least eat something?" he asked.

Kitty laughed lightly. "I doubt Annie will starve her, papa."

"Annie and Little J are my youngest daughters, Captain Aubrey," Sebastian explained to him. "Annie was married little over a year ago to our reverend and lives about a mile from us."

Captain Aubrey looked up from his breakfast and smiled at her father. Kitty couldn't help but like the way his face crinkled when he smiled. It made him look a lot nicer then when he blatantly stared and 'observed' as he put it. "I gather 'Little J' is not her Christian name?"

"She is named for my sister, Jane," Sebastian clarified. "Just as Kitty is named for my mother. It got too confusing for the girls when they were young so 'Kitty' and 'Little J' stuck. I doubt they'll ever go back to Catherine and Jane."

Kitty knew she would never go back to using the name 'Catherine'. She didn't like it; it made her sound too old. She much preferred her nickname. Little J on the other hand ... she would always be known as Little J but Kitty knew that sometimes she was tired of it.

Kitty caught her brother's eye as she reached for the jam. He was staring at her deviously as he subtly gestured Captain Aubrey suggestively. It angered her to know that he brother was informed of her parent's intentions regarding Captain Aubrey. She smiled slightly as she scooped some jam onto her knife. As she did so she jumped in her seat and the jam went flying and landed directly on top of Captain Aubrey's head.

Kitty bit her lip to stop herself from laughing. In her defence, she was aiming for James; perhaps it was what Captain Aubrey deserved.

"Kitty!" her father exclaimed. "What on earth is the matter with you? Captain Aubrey, I do apologise, Kitty is probably just sleep deprived from all the dancing last night."

Captain Aubrey used his napkin to wipe away the jam that was running through his dark blonde hair. "No need to worry, Lord Ethridge, there is no harm done," he said in an annoyed tone. Kitty happened to catch a quick glare that he sent her way.

"Kitty," her mother hissed under her breath. "Apologise."

Kitty rolled her eyes and plastered on a fake, yet sympathetic smile. "Forgive me, Captain, as papa said, I am sleep deprived." She smiled sweetly at him. James poorly disguised a laugh as a cough.

"No need to apologise, Lady Kitty, I can tell it was an accident," Captain Aubrey replied icily. Kitty had to admit one thing; he was right when he said he could see through people, as he saw through her quite easily.

"Kitty, go and show Captain Aubrey where the bell is so that he may have a bath brought up for him," her father urged.

Kitty pouted. "Why can't we just ask one of the footmen?" she asked impatiently. "They're right outside waiting for us to finish."

Sebastian sent his daughter a warning look and she knew to hold her tongue. "Do it now, Kitty."

Kitty rose from her seat silently and walked around the dining table to Captain Aubrey's side. "If you'll follow me, I will show you where the bell is," Kitty said glumly.

"I'd be happy to," Captain Aubrey said in the same tone as he rose as well. He followed her from the dining room and into the hallway.

Kitty made her way straight to the corner of the hallway where the bell rope resided.

"Your aim surpasses my expectations, Lady Kitty," Captain Aubrey commented as they walked.

Kitty sucked in a breath. She didn't want to raise her voice or say anything horrid when her parents might hear. "For your information," she said calmly. "I was aiming for my brother. It was not my fault that your fat head got in the way!"

Pure fury flashed across his bright, blue eyes. "Do you know what I would have done to one of men if they'd just spoken to me with such a lack of respect as you've just done?"

"Pray tell," Kitty said sarcastically. She could see that he was trying to calm himself as his shoulders were rising and falling slower.

He pursed his lips for a moment before talking. "There was once a Greek queen called Cassiopeia, who was incredibly beautiful," he told her suddenly.

Kitty furrowed her eyebrows. "What does that have to do with anything?" she asked. Wasn't he about to tell her what horrid punishments he handed out to members of his crew if they disrespected him?

"Cassiopeia was famed for her beauty but infamous for her vanity, arrogance and conceit. Would you like to know what happened to Cassiopeia?" he asked in a thoughtful tone.

Kitty knew he was using the story of a probably fake queen as a metaphor for herself. And she did not appreciate it. "Why not?" she muttered.

"She infuriated the God, Poseidon, so he punished her. She was tied to a throne and condemned to be a constellation for the rest of her life, and because of her position in the sky she was upside down so that all her blood rushed to her big head."

"Are you saying that I'm like Cassiopeia?" Kitty demanded to know. She was neither vain nor arrogant. She was never conceited. She knew she was beautiful but only because she was told so very often. The fact of her beauty did not warrant her condemning.

Captain Aubrey feigned ignorance. "I was just talking about Greek mythology, what you make of it is up to you."

Kitty huffed impatiently and turned to yank on the bell harder than usual. "I suppose Cassiopeia loved going to parties and jilting her partners, too, then?" she quipped angrily.

Captain Aubrey simply smiled at her. It gave Kitty pleasure that she could still see the redness from the strawberry jam still in his hair. "I never said Cassiopeia was anything like you … but now that you draw the comparison, I can see it. I'd steer clear of any thrones if I were you."

"How dare you!" Kitty gasped and the rudeness of the guest. She may have been just a silly woman but she still deserved respect.

"I mean no disrespect Cassio ... er ... Kitty – my mistake. Forgive me, Lady Kitty, it was one easy to make," he smiled comically at her.

He was teasing her. Kitty couldn't think of anything smart to say back to him so she only turned on her heel and walked off from him. "I hope your bath water burns you!" she shouted over her shoulder, no longer caring who heard her. "I am not, nor will I ever be Cassiopeia," she whispered to herself.

Chapter 3

Kitty spent the better part of the day getting ready for the military salute at Sir Walter Martin's residence. She wanted to look her best regardless of what Captain Aubrey had insinuated. Looking beautiful was not a crime and it certainly did not mean she was condemned to the sky.

A maid helped her with her long brown hair, making what were unkempt curls into a lovely braided up – do with a few loose tendrils hanging by her face. Her gown was a beautiful ivory colour and the seam had been dropped to the waist as the fashions changed. She enjoyed the new waistline better as it showed off the ladies figures rather than them seeming ambiguous with the seams being under the bust. The only negative was the tighter corsets so that waistlines appeared smaller.

Once the maid had been dismissed Kitty took a good look at herself in the mirror. She'd never thought of herself as a vain person. She'd always been grateful that she'd been fortunate looking. She pinched her cheeks a few times to redden them a little before standing up. She thought the time to leave would be arriving soon.

As she stood there was a knock on the door. "Can I come in?" Sabine asked from the other side of the door.

"Yes," Kitty called back.

Sabine entered the room looking very uncomfortable. She sat down immediately on Kitty's bed and took some deep breaths. "Why must my waist be cinched so?" she complained and laid her head back on the bed.

"Do not ruin your hair, Sabine!" Kitty said warily. Sabine immediately sat back up rolling her eyes.

"At home I braid my hair myself in the morning and mama does not fret about it," she moaned and rubbed her corseted waist.

Kitty smiled at her elder cousin. "If it makes you feel any better, you look stunning." It was the truth. Sabine was oblivious to her beauty and often denied it. Her hair was effortlessly shiny and she didn't need rags to keep it curly which Kitty envied. Every night she had rags digging into the back of her neck and it severely irritated her.

Sabine scoffed. "If you say so," she said in disbelief. "I don't know how you manage all these parties, I am so tired!"

It suddenly hit Kitty that Sabine was absent from breakfast that morning. "I suppose mama allowed you to sleep this morning?" she asked knowingly.

"I'm grateful to Aunt Em for allowing me to sleep, I needed it," she smirked. "But I do wish I could be home. I know men find me boring here."

Kitty knew that was true. Sabine was not boring as a person once you got to know her, she was kind and generous and knowledgeable ... it was just that the men during the London season appreciated the girls that liked to laugh and were forthcoming with their affections … something that Sabine was definitely not.

"Why don't you like dancing, Sabine? If you relaxed a little you might find someone who catches your eye," Kitty urged positively, joining her cousin on the bed.

Sabine threw Kitty and exasperated look. "I like dancing," she sighed. "I guess I'm just not that confident around London society, I feel as though they are scrutinising my every move. Every time I dance with a man that a fine lady had her eye on for her daughter I hear whispers about me. I feel as though I'm not good enough."

Kitty pouted. "Not good enough? Sabine, you're an Earl's daughter! You would be a fine match for any man," she assured her. She knew it for she had received quite a few offers during her seasons.

Sabine smiled thankfully towards Kitty. "And it is usually me trying to make you see rationally," she laughed lightly.

Kitty nodded in agreement. "Who knew it would be me that was the logical one," she winked.

"I received a letter from mama today," Sabine said in a slightly annoyed tone. "They've hired another stable hand – a Scotsman."

Kitty knew how fond her cousin was of her horse. They had an amazing bond. It was obvious when she visited how much Sabine and Puissant trusted each other. "A Scotsman?" Kitty raised her eyebrows. "What's he doing in England, I wonder?"

Sabine shrugged her shoulders. "His name is Mr McKenzie and apparently he was hired after he caught Puissant after she broke free of the stables."

"Well that's a good thing, then, isn't it?" Kitty thought aloud. "If he hadn't been there Puissant could have been halfway to Wales before they even knew she was missing."

"I know in my head that what you're saying is logical but I just wish I was home looking after her. I wouldn't care if I never received an offer, I'd rather spend time in my stable," Sabine sighed.

Kitty lightly slapped Sabine on the back as she rose from the bed. "Come now, we will not dwell on what we once had ... for example I'm choosing not to dwell on the fact that I have an incompetent naval captain living in my house who enjoys talking about utter nonsense," Kitty growled under her breath. "Have you ever heard of Cassiopeia?" she asked her cousin.

Sabine nodded. "I learnt about her during lessons when I was younger," she replied. "Why do you ask?"

Kitty furrowed her eyebrows. "Why on earth would you learn about a vain queen during lessons?"

Sabine shrugged. "I didn't actually learn that Cassiopeia was named after a vain queen until later on, I first learnt about the constellation. Mama felt guilty that Philip and Louis were able to attend Eton so she designed a similar curriculum for me," she replied simply. "I learnt about history, geography, literature, arithmetic and all sorts of religions, it was quite interesting. And then of course I would go outside and spend the rest of the day in the stables."

Kitty was amazed. When she was in the schoolroom she learnt about languages, music, drawing and dancing. She could embroider and play the pianoforte but she couldn't do much else. It never occurred to her to demand a more extensive education. She didn't think about what her brother's were learning when they went away to school; she just sat with her sisters and learnt what her governess told her. "Perhaps he's right about me," Kitty whispered under her breath.

"Who's right about you?" Sabine asked.

Kitty realised that she probably hadn't whispered quietly. "Captain Aubrey," she replied. "He said he wasn't insinuating anything, but I knew he was making parallels between Cassiopeia and I. Do you think me so shallow?"

Sabine looked alarmed. "Absolutely not, Kitty," she assured her. "Yes, you can be a little outspoken sometimes but if a man can't handle a woman who speaks her mind then he doesn't deserve her company. But you're a beautiful person, Kitty. You're a dear friend and cousin to me, and I value your counsel." Sabine took Kitty's hand reassuringly.

"Even if my counsel is outspoken?" Kitty giggled.

"I prefer it that way," Sabine winked. "Don't ever change for a man, Kitty. I may have little experience in that area, but a woman should never change who she is to suit a man. Cassiopeia might've been vain, but she said what she believed. It was a man who condemned her after all. She believed she was the most beautiful of them all ... perhaps Poseidon asked to court her and she refused."

Kitty burst out laughing and pulled her cousin from the bed. "Thank you, Sabine," she said, still laughing as she pulled her into a hug. "You've made my outlook on this evening even better. Let's go and have some fun. Stay near Evangeline and I this evening, we won't let you experience any boredom, I promise you."

Sabine linked arms with Kitty as they both walked out of Kitty's bedchamber. "I trust you, Kitty," she said warily. "Don't get me into any trouble."

"I won't," Kitty rolled her eyes. "With any luck I'll have you engaged before the night is out. I don't want you going home unattached. If that Scotsman sees you are unmarried he won't be able to control himself!"

Sabine scoffed at her younger cousin. "Don't be absurd. He won't be a young man. What young man leaves his country? He's probably a widower like my father was and looking for a new lease on life in England."

Kitty conceded. "You're right, he's probably old and ugly," she shrugged. "Come on, let's go downstairs and see if we are all ready to go. I wonder if Little J's back," Kitty suddenly realised that her younger sister hadn't returned from wherever she'd scampered off to that morning.

"Where did she go?" Sabine asked.

Kitty shook her head. "I don't know. She disappears every morning and returns before dinner. I have to tell mama and papa that's she's at Annie's or is at church of is in the park. It's been going on for awhile now ... come to think of it, a long time. I hope she isn't in trouble." Kitty wished that

Little J would confide in her, lord knows that Little J knew everything about Kitty.

"She won't be," Sabine shook off the notion. "Little J's too clever to do anything stupid. If she'd been born a boy and attended Eton and Cambridge, I guarantee you she would be the next prime minister."

"You're right," Kitty nodded.

They both walked downstairs to find her family accumulating their last minute belongings before they set off for Sir Walter Martin's ball. Kitty noticed that Captain Aubrey was having a light hearted conversation with her father.

He did look very handsome dressed in his naval uniform. His navy coat was perfectly presented and it fitted him exactly. The brass buttons shone and the golden trim on his jacket made him look very regal even though he was not technically a member of the ton. He turned to look at her suddenly and furrowed his eyebrows.

"Kitty?" her father said loudly.

Kitty's head snapped up and she looked to her father. "Yes?"

"I asked if you'd seen Little J above stairs," he said slowly. "Are you feeling alright?"

Kitty's cheeks reddened much to her embarrassment. She must've looked like a complete illiterate when her father had asked the question and she had appeared oblivious ... and staring at Captain Aubrey.

"I'm quite alright ... no, Little J wasn't upstairs, she must still be at church," Kitty replied quickly, trying to divert the attention away from herself.

Sebastian furrowed his eyebrows. "I thought you said she went to Annie's this morning?"

Kitty froze. She'd just ruined whatever her sister was doing.

"She was, papa, she was going to Annie's and then to the church," James said smoothly.

Kitty could sometimes detest her twin brother, but he knew how to defuse a situation.

"It's not very polite of her to be late to a function," her mother said disapprovingly. "I'll have to talk to her in the morning. I don't like her crossing town every day, it's not safe. You should really make sure she is chaperoned. We're too laissez-faire as parents, especially with the girls."

Kitty could have slapped Captain Aubrey when a small smirk appeared on his face as her mother spoke those words. "Mama, Little J is responsible and clever, she doesn't need a chaperone. You're not too lenient as parents, you've been good. Look at James, he's studying at Oxford!"

James looked startled at the mention of his education. When he'd announced he wanted to study at Oxford his father was very happy that he wanted to mature. Even though he was attending school, his womanising behaviour had not changed, hence his punishment.

"Thank you, dear," her mother smiled. "I appreciate it. Alright, no more waiting, we don't want to be the last one's to arrive, let's go."

Within ten minutes their carriage was pulling up outside Sir Walter Martin's house. It wasn't as fine as the manor houses that the lords and ladies resided in but it was still a nice house. It was large enough to host a military salute, after all.

As Kitty was helped from the carriage she marvelled at the number of naval officers surrounding her. It was the first time that she'd ever attended a military salute that was for the navy. From the corner of her eye she watched as Captain Aubrey joined his men and guided them inside.

Kitty followed her parents inside and the announcer took their names and titles.

"Lord Sebastian Alcott, Earl of Ethridge," cried the announcer as her father entered. "Lady Emilia Alcott, Countess of Ethridge." Both her parents then descended the stairs into the ballroom.

Her brother then gave his name to the announcer who promptly called out his name.

"The Honourable James Alcott, eldest son of Lord and Lady Ethridge." James quickly walked down the stairs to join her parents.

Kitty then walked up to the announcer.

"Your name, milady?" he asked.

"Lady Catherine Alcott, eldest daughter of Lord and Lady Ethridge," she replied as he handed her a stiff, white dance card.

He smiled at her. "Walk on down, milady," he instructed. "Lady Catherine Alcott, eldest daughter of Lord and Lady Ethridge," he called out to the room.

Kitty reviewed the list of dances as she reached the bottom of the stairs. Her favourite dance, the quadrille, was the second dance to be played. She hoped to have a desirable partner for that dance. As the quadrille was the most popular dance, she often had men asking her to dance it even when she didn't want to do it with them.

"Lady Sabine Winchester, eldest daughter of Lord and Lady Southerby," cried the announcer as Sabine entered the dance.

Kitty waited for Sabine to join her and they both walked into the crowd of people. Within minutes more than half of her dance card was filled but she was grateful that the first few dances remained vacant. Sabine too had quite a few offers that she timidly accepted.

After about twenty minutes an impeccably groomed Evangeline hugged her tightly. "You look magnificent!" she exclaimed

Kitty giggled as she received her friend. "As do you, Eva," Kitty smiled. Evangeline did look exceptionally beautiful. Her blonde hair was swept up into a pretty knot and her gown was a lovely shade of blue that showed off her very narrow figure. "You know my cousin, Sabine?" Kitty asked pulling Sabine forward.

Evangeline nodded. "Yes, we met the other night," she smiled. "You look ravishing also, Sabine, a fine prize for any man wanting to take you at the end of the season."

Sabine blushed. "I doubt it, but thank you," she replied bashfully.

"Well," Evangeline sighed. "I'll have to love you and leave you; I'm wanted for the first dance. Be on the lookout for Sir Walter, word is that he still has his eyes on you." With that

Evangeline disappeared back into the crowd and Sabine and Kitty were left alone.

Kitty looked around the room and was relieved when she didn't see Sir Walter anywhere. "Come Sabine, I will show you how I enjoy an evening during the summer."

Between dances Kitty took Sabine to the refreshments table and enjoyed more than their fair share of champagne. Kitty made sure that nobody was looking directly at her and Sabine when they drank. It was very unladylike of her to have more than one glass but she was tired of being a lady. She was taking Sabine's advice – she was never going to change to suit anyone other than herself.

She had a severe case of the giggles by the time she drank her fourth glass. Sabine too, which was incredibly out of character for her, seemed very light hearted.

It was after midnight when the band was having an interlude that someone tapped her on the shoulder.

Kitty spun around to see Sir Walter Martin standing before her expectantly. He was a portly man who enjoyed a good meal. His black hair was neatly slicked back and his neat beard had been freshly trimmed. His steel grey eyes surveyed Kitty with lust. "The next dance, if you please, Lady Kitty," he asked politely.

Kitty, in her drunken stupor, burst into a fit of giggles. She noticed eyes on her but it didn't occur to her that is was a negative thing. "But you're so old, Sir Walter!" she laughed.

Sir Walter looked taken aback at Kitty's brazen statement. "I beg your pardon?"

Kitty continued laughing. "Beg all you like, I won't dance with you," she said casually and turned away from him. "Come on Sabine, let's go and find Eva." She linked arms with her cousin but before they could go anywhere she was pulled in another direction by a pair of hands that were completely foreign to her. She looked up to see a very angry looking Captain Aubrey. "Captain Aubrey," she sniggered. "Did you know that I would think you handsome if you weren't such a prude?"

He didn't answer or look down at her. He only continued walking. Before she knew it she was standing before her parents who looked startled to see her standing there.

"Captain Aubrey?" her father asked, confused.

Her mother pulled her from Captain Aubrey's arms and supported her weight. "Good lord, Kitty, what is wrong with you?" she demanded to know.

"Lord Ethridge, I appreciate the invitation and the insinuation that there is to be a union between Lady Kitty and me, but I'm afraid I must refuse. I mean no disrespect to you, milord, but your daughter makes herself and those around her ridiculous! She is out of control and I would urge you to make her change before she ruins herself and your good name."

Kitty's eyes widened as she listened to the words that were coming out of Captain Aubrey's mouth. She had been called many things in her time in society, mainly beautiful and elegant ... but she'd never been called 'ridiculous'.

Sebastian writhed in anger. "I would ask you to hold your tongue, young man. You are speaking of my daughter," he spat.

"She just humiliated a perfect gentleman!" he said exasperatedly. "And she's had at least four glasses of champagne. She needs a leash before she's thrown out of London as a common tramp."

Sebastian's eyes widened in shock. "What?"

"Four glasses, Kitty?" Emilia asked in disbelief. "And you said we weren't too lenient," she growled. "Sebastian go and give our goodbyes, I want to leave."

"Milord," Captain Aubrey said in a calmer voice. "I do not speak ill of Lady Kitty for my own entertainment; I mean only to warn you. Control her or risk her silly behaviour ruining you all."

Kitty glared at the Captain. "I am right here, you know," she snapped. "I can hear what you're saying. Stop speaking rubbish!"

"Em, put Kitty in the carriage, I'll collect the boys and Sabine," Sebastian said angrily. "I trust you'll be departing our house, Captain?"

Captain Aubrey nodded. "I received a missive detailing our departure timetable. We'll be away by the end of the week." He met Kitty's hateful glare with a sincere look that surprised her. "I'd hate to see another fallen woman be laughed out of London, Lady Kitty. Believe me, I know. I'm doing this for your own good."

Kitty didn't know what to say or think. She let her mother lead her away from the ballroom and out of Sir Walter's house.

"Honestly, Kitty, I thought it was Little J I had to worry about. Is Captain Aubrey right? Are you a fallen woman?" her mother asked in a worried voice.

Kitty's eyes widened. "No, mama," she replied. "I'm not fallen." Only broken.

Chapter 4

As soon as Kitty had been left alone in her bedchamber she took it as a chance to escape. She just wanted out of her house. She didn't want to have to face her parent's disappointed expressions.

As she stole down the staircase stepping a silently as possible she was stopped by the same man that had ratted her out to her parents in the first place.

"Where do you think you're going?" he asked.

Kitty should have been wary as she had been caught once again doing something that she shouldn't have done. "Out," she said poisonously.

Captain Aubrey smiled at her slightly. Kitty didn't know what he was doing up and still completely dressed in his naval uniform but she wasn't about to start a complete conversation about it with him. "I know you think I'm the enemy, Kitty, but time will tell you that I've helped you. You will thank me for it one day," he said confidently.

Kitty arched her eyebrows. "Don't hold your breath ... or do," she snapped and went to push past him on the stairs but he caught her upper arm. There was always a feeling of hesitation whenever she was touched by another man, but it didn't feel wrong which she cursed herself for.

"Lady Kitty, walk with me," he commanded. He offered her his arm which she felt obligated to take. He led her down the stairs and out into the courtyard that she had seen him standing in on the night of her family's ball. He looked up at the stars like she had seen him do before and sighed. "There was once a woman named Frances Hepburn. She was beautiful, more beautiful than any other woman that was being presented to society. Everyone thought that she had been born to be a duchess. But Frances fell; she was seduced by a man who she thought loved her. There she was, seventeen and with child, and completely ruined."

Kitty's eyes widened. "What happened to her?" she whispered.

"She was sent by her parents to have the child in the country at her grandparent's residence. Once the child was born she was sent Paris and lived the remainder of her life in a convent," Captain Aubrey replied, still looking at the stars.

"And the child?" she prompted.

"He was fine. He was raised by farmers in the local village. He grew up happy and healthy and joined the navy when he was old enough and went up through the ranks until he was Captain," he smiled looking down at her.

Kitty's eyes widened with realisation. Captain Aubrey knew exactly what happened to women when they were ruined. He was the product of a woman being ruined. She didn't know what to say to him.

"You needn't say anything, it's not a story I tell very often," he smiled at her, as if he had read her mind. "I see women like you whenever we make port. Lively and enthusiastic, and I just can't help but fear that what happened to my mother will happen to you. It is a warning, Lady Kitty. You don't deserve extradition."

Kitty could finally see why he had behaved the way he had around her. He was being genuine. He wasn't deliberately trying to cause friction between her and her parents; he was trying to prevent the inevitable if she had gone on behaving how she was. "Why do you keep looking at the sky?" Kitty finally asked.

Captain Aubrey smiled widely. "It comforts me, I suppose. I look up to it, wherever I am in the world, and it looks the same. It eases the homesickness."

"Where are you going when you depart?" she wondered aloud.

"We're heading west, towards the Caribbean," he replied. "His Majesty's ships are needed to make sure the trade route is safe. We've had a few altercations with pirates, I'm afraid."

Kitty gasped. "Pirates! Won't that be dangerous?" she asked desperately. She'd read about pirates ... or Little J had read about them and then conveyed her findings to her elder sister. Nevertheless they were ruthless and cunning individuals who ploughed and plumaged whatever they came across.

Captain Aubrey laughed lightly. "Is that concern I hear in your voice?"

Kitty's eyes narrowed. "I wouldn't want such a fine ship to be sent to the bottom of the ocean," she snapped quickly.

He rolled his eyes. "Any journey involves danger, Lady Kitty, and yes, this one will be particularly dangerous, but it's nothing that we can't handle."

"Well," she sighed. "I wish you luck. May you be back home before you know it, looking up into English skies." Kitty resisted telling him that she hoped he saw Cassiopeia in the sky because she wanted that person to be forgotten.

Captain Aubrey nodded in thanks. "I appreciate that, Lady Kitty," he said gratefully. "I hope that in my absence you will be wary. I find myself worrying about you. I know I've only just met you but since I've experienced your behaviour I worry when you are out of my sight. I don't want to see what happened to my mother happen to you."

Kitty wore a puzzled expression on her face. "Can I ask why I am any concern of yours?"

Captain Aubrey looked down at her with his piercing blue eyes that stood out so prominently in the cool night. "Why should you not be? You are a good young woman and you don't have to behave like you do to be noticed. You do that quite effortlessly anyway."

Kitty furrowed her eyebrows. Had he just insulted her or had he just complimented her? "Thank you?" she answered as if it were a question.

"All I ask is that you're careful, Lady Kitty," he said sincerely.

Kitty rubbed her arms to warm herself. There was a cool breeze blowing throughout the streets of London that was quite nippy. "Now is that concern I hear, Captain Aubrey?" Kitty chirped, using his own words against him.

"Yes," he replied simply. "It is concern. You should probably go back upstairs and go to bed, instead of sneaking off to wherever you were planning. I can imagine that your parents will want words with you in the morning. I do apologise for what I said, it was harsh and reflecting back on it I do wish I hadn't been so blunt."

"So you don't think me ridiculous?" Kitty said distastefully.

"I think what you did to Sir Walter was ridiculous, Lady Kitty, I won't take that back. But I do take back what I said about you being out of control. I do believe you to be energetic, Lady Kitty, but I also believe you to be capable of change." Captain Aubrey let out a sad sigh.

"Change is such an ambiguous word," Kitty told him as she turned back towards the door. "You can never know whether it will be good or bad."

Captain Aubrey didn't look at her when she spoke. "However uncertain we are, we cannot evolve without change."

Kitty nodded even though he could not see her. "Sleep well, Captain. Pray you do not wake up to my parents scolding me at the top of their lungs."

Captain Aubrey chuckled quietly. "My prayers are ever changing, Lady Kitty. It seems I have something new to ask God for when I sleep tonight."

Kitty didn't ask what he meant by it, as she wasn't sure she wanted to know the answer. She didn't understand how he could be so angry and then so tender at the same time. She was intrigued by Captain Aubrey, but for the life of her she didn't know why.

Kitty felt as though she'd been trampled by a horse when she awoke the next morning. It wasn't because of the fact that she'd consumed more champagne than she usually had, or that because she was embarrassed, she was just hurt. She was hurt by the fact that her parents were disappointed in her. And she was hurt by the fact that Captain Aubrey was right. She knew he was right about her, and she knew she had to change.

"Kitty," Emilia called through the door as she knocked. "I'm coming in." She opened the door as Kitty sat up in bed. Her mother was still wearing her nightdress and her hair was just in a simple braid.

"Mama," Kitty said in a timid tone.

Emilia sat down on the end of the bed and looked at her daughter sadly. "I don't know what to say to you. I've always seen you as sensible and proper, I haven't needed to worry about you or to make sure you were chaperoned at every minute of every day."

Kitty looked down at her hands and sighed. "Are you very angry at me?" she asked quietly.

"I'm disappointed," she replied. "Papa and I are disappointed."

"That's worse than angry," Kitty whispered.

"Kitty, you are a good person. You don't need to be silly to get attention; you get enough attention as it is. You always have eyes on you darling," her mother said honestly.

Kitty couldn't help but think of what Captain Aubrey had said to her the night before, about her getting attention without trying. "Mama, I know I went a little far last night, but I don't want you to be disappointed in me," Kitty looked up at her mother hopefully. It hurt her to see her mother frowning at her.

"Those words that Captain Aubrey spoke last night really shocked me, Kitty," she sighed. "But I know I owe him my gratitude because it was true, you could have been laughed out of London if he had not intervened last night. I won't have one of my daughters fall if I can save her."

"Mama, I've not fallen. I'm as pure as the day I was born," Kitty assured her mother.

Emilia smiled slightly. "I remember that day as if it were yesterday. You and your brother were so perfect; I couldn't have loved you any more if I tried."

Kitty felt tears flooding her eyes. "Mama, I'm sorry," she whispered.

Emilia stood up from the foot of the bed and she knelt down next to Kitty so that she could wrap her arms around her. "I know," she sighed and kissed the side of her head. "But you can understand why we want you to change, can't you? You might think that your behaviour is harmless but these society women can be brutal, trust me, I know."

Kitty cocked her head to the side. "How do you know that?" she asked.

"Because they spoke about me when I married papa," she replied.

Kitty bit her lip. Her parents had never discussed the circumstances of their marriage. She'd never asked why her mother's skin was marred or why her father was Earl when his father was a farmer. She'd just let it be, figuring that they would tell her and her siblings whenever they were ready.

"Why did they speak about you?" Kitty whispered.

Emilia motioned for Kitty to move over in the bed which she did. She climbed in next to her and placed an arm around her shoulders.

"None of your siblings know this, and I don't want them to know. But I will tell you that before papa and I married I was married to a horrendous man. He was very cruel to me ... I won't go into details ... but in public he was a perfect gentleman. So when I married your father so soon after he died there were whispers that Sebastian and I had had an affair, that we'd dishonoured the good Alcott name. There was even a rumour that I killed Vincent to marry your father. I know what it is like to be the subject of gossip Kitty, and I don't want that for you."

Kitty's jaw dropped as she listened. She could never have imagined it. Vincent was his name. She wouldn't ask, as she already knew, but Vincent had done those awful things to her mother's skin. Vincent was his name. She knew that he wasn't welcomed into heaven.

"Mama, why would you not tell us this?" she asked quietly.

Emilia's brown eyes saddened. "I like to pretend that that period of my life never happened," she replied simply. "Your father was the best thing that could have ever happened to me. And then you five came along in quick succession and I felt like I'd had to endure all that with Vincent so that I could be so happy with my family." Her arms tightened around Kitty. "One day when you're a mother you'll understand why

I'm so worried about you, about all of you. To save you from harm … Kitty, I'd throw myself under a carriage for you or slice off my own arm."

Kitty smiled. "From now on, mama, I'm going to behave. I'll be completely proper. Captain Aubrey, as much as he can irritate me, what he said to me makes sense." The first thing she was going to do when she was at another ball was apologise to Sir Walter Martin.

Emilia kissed Kitty's forehead. "Captain Aubrey is fond of you. Even though he spoke of you harshly, I could tell that deep down inside it was because he was worried."

Kitty resisted smiling knowingly. He has said so himself that he worried. "Mama, Captain Aubrey is not fond of me. He's just noble. He's a leader and so he protects."

Kitty could practically hear her mother rolling her eyes. "So long as he protects you then I'm satisfied. I don't think your father will be as easy on you as I was, he will probably demand that you remain at his side for any further outings, just like James."

Kitty groaned. "Very well," she conceded. "But am I at least able to dance if I am asked?"

Emilia got out of Kitty's bed and walked over to the door. "I'm sure papa will allow you if the right person asks."

Kitty knew exactly who she meant and she was sure that he would never ask. "I doubt it, mama," she sighed.

"Breakfast is in half an hour, don't be late," she said as she left the room.

Kitty climbed out of bed and went to sit down at her dresser. As she undid the braids in her hair she smiled at herself in the mirror. "I'm going to change," she said to herself. "I won't be condemned to the sky or to a Parisian convent."

Chapter 5

K itty was very nervous as she went down to breakfast. Her relationship with her mother was still alright but she wasn't sure how her father would feel. He was very protective of all his children. Most fathers would not care if their sons went off and enjoyed women but he did, and James was being punished for it. So, she too would be punished for behaving poorly in public, and she was not looking forward to it.

One of the footmen opened the dining room door for her and she entered carefully.

The men, being her father, brothers and Captain Aubrey all stood. Her mother, Sabine and Little J looked at her cautiously.

"Good morning," Kitty said quietly. She met Captain Aubrey's encouraging eyes as she sat down next to Little J beside her mother.

"Catherine," her father said gruffly. "I trust you slept well." Kitty knew she was in trouble if he was using her Christian name.

"Yes, papa," she nodded. Nobody dared start helping themselves to the breakfast foods laid out for them. Fresh bread and butter, steaming scones and jam, ham, eggs and cheeses as well as their tea and milk all sat untouched.

Little J took Kitty's hand under the table and squeezed it reassuringly.

"Mama tells me that you've promised to behave," he said tensely.

Kitty looked up at her father for the first time. His dark blue eyes, the colour that mirrored her eyes, were very serious. "I have, papa," she nodded. "I'm sorry if I've embarrassed you or caused you any shame. It was unconsciously done. I now know that sometimes change is what we need to evolve," she told him, stealing a glance at Captain Aubrey. He was smiling ever so slightly at her. She could have sworn he looked proud.

Sebastian seemed to ponder her words for a moment. "I want you by my side until I'm convinced, Kitty," he said calmly. "We've received an invitation for a dinner party as Lady Russel's this evening. It's not a formal assembly, it is just a dinner. So you will sit by me so I can keep an eye on you. I believe that Sir Walter will be there as he is a friend of the Russel's so you will have an opportunity to apologise to him then."

Kitty nodded. "I will, papa," she promised. She knew that Sir Walter deserved an apology. She should not have treated him so horribly. She may not be romantically interested in him but she should not have encouraged his affections if she was sure she would not want them in the end.

Sebastian smiled, satisfied. "Alright, everyone eat before it gets cold, there's nothing worse than lukewarm tea."

Once everyone began filling their plates with breakfast, Little J nudged her sister. "What on earth did you get up to last night?" she whispered.

Kitty turned to her younger sister as she cracked the shell on her egg. "Let's just say that I'm no longer going to be the centre of attention at balls. Where were you last night? Papa was wondering."

Little J bit her lip awkwardly. "I stayed at Annie's late," she so obviously lied. '

Kitty rolled her eyes. "I'm sure you were," she said, pretending to go along.

"Little J," her father called down the table. Both Little J and Kitty turned to their father expectantly.

"Yes, papa?"

"Do you have any expeditions planned today?" he asked as he took a sip from his teacup.

Little J nodded. "I was planning on going to Hyde Park and reading," she replied.

Kitty's eyes flashed to James' whose eyes immediately rolled.

"Do you know that I haven't spent the day at the park for a long while," Emilia said enthusiastically. "Captain Aubrey, have you ever been to Hyde Park?"

Captain Aubrey placed his fork back on his plate and shook his head. "No, I'm afraid I haven't spent much time in London."

"That settles it then, I'll have the cook prepare us a basket and we'll spend the day at the park. We'll be home in time to change and be ready for Lady Russel's dinner party," Emilia clapped her hands excitedly.

Little J pouted. "But mama, I wanted to spend the day lost in a book, perhaps we should go to the park another day," she urged.

Kitty smirked, knowing what her mother was organising was interfering with her plans.

"Little J, you spend every day getting lost in a book, if you're not careful you'll start to look like one," Henry quipped.

"Hush, Henry," Emilia snapped. "Little J, you will spend a day with your family, please, we never see you." Emilia's word was final, Little J could not argue.

Little J conceded and nodded.

By the time everyone had finished eating and had gathered their belongings to go out, it was after noon.

Kitty had donned her white bonnet and shawl to compliment her pale pink gown. Her long brown hair was combed to its natural straight appearance and was hanging down her back instead of being pinned on top of her head.

Instead of ordering the carriage, they'd all decided to walk to Hyde Park. Her parents took the lead with her father carrying the picnic basket filled with their lunch. Following them were her two brothers and then Sabine and Little J. Captain Aubrey hung back so that he could walk alongside her. Kitty wished that her father had ordered the carriage as it was quite warm and all the ladies were wearing several layers of fabric.

"You disobey your father already, Lady Kitty?" he asked in an amused tone.

Kitty rolled her eyes, realising what he was meaning. "I don't think he means I have to be by his side every second of every day." Kitty noticed how he was wearing a more informal uniform during the day. He was still wearing a navy coloured coat with lovely brass buttons, but he wasn't wearing any of the fine decorations that she was sure were reserved for fancy balls.

"You look very lovely today, Lady Kitty," he complimented sincerely, offering his arm to her formally.

A light blush tinted Kitty's cheeks as she accepted his arm. "Thank you," she said quietly.

"I like you hair like that, I've always found that natural is best," he smiled.

Kitty liked his face when he smiled, it made him seem human and not like some unemotional military man. His face creased up and he looked very relaxed. "It is more comfortable then having a thousand pins stuck in my head. It is less time consuming also." Subconsciously she played with a section of her hair with her spare hand.

"Are you nervous about tonight?" he asked.

Kitty shook her head. "It may surprise you, Captain, but I have some experience with talking," she grinned at him.

"Will your friend be in attendance tonight? You know the one with the blonde hair?" he asked curiously.

Kitty's eyes widened. He'd been lecturing her about changing when Evangeline was just as bad, if not worse than her. "Lady Evangeline is not in the same circle as Lady Russel," she replied curtly.

Captain Aubrey smiled, much to Kitty's surprise. "Good, she's a little too ... loquacious for my liking. Of course I haven't spoken to her personally but I've seen her in action," he chuckled.

Kitty realised that she'd just overreacted, but why she couldn't be sure. She needn't worry anyway; Evangeline would never fancy a man like Captain Aubrey as he didn't have a title or a fancy house. "What is your ship called, Captain Aubrey?" Kitty asked wanting to change the subject.

"The vessel is named 'Royal Rose'. I think she was named after the King's niece, Victoria, in honour of her birth," Captain Aubrey replied. "It does not sound fearsome but she has a hundred and twenty guns."

"A hundred and twenty?" Kitty gasped in disbelief. "Why on earth would one ship need so many guns?"

"It is a military ship, Lady Kitty, what did you think it was for?" he asked curiously.

Kitty bit her lip nervously. "I don't know, I suppose one forgets that great battles occur outside of out perfect little world in the ton. Call it naivety," she shrugged.

By then the party had arrived at the park. Several couples and families were making their way around the park engaged in conversation. There were also several groups of people sitting on blankets under the beautiful oak trees enjoying their luncheon outdoors.

"Did you know that my mother and father got engaged in Hyde Park?" Kitty asked Captain Aubrey as her mother began setting out the blanket so they could all sit down.

"It seems like a very tranquil place, especially with the water," he replied, smiling. "My mother and father ... my adopted mother and father, got engaged in a similar place back home, of course it is not as grand as Hyde Park but it has the same ambience."

"Where are you from, Captain?" Kitty asked curiously. She was aware her family could hear them now she wasn't going to discuss anything incriminating, for example the fact that Captain Aubrey was a bastard child.

"Yes, Captain, we haven't heard the story of how you came to be, enlighten us," Emilia chimed in as she unpacked the picnic basket. She laid out several plates of cold meats and cheeses as well as fresh fruit and wine. Kitty enjoyed such informal family outings when she didn't have to have such rigid posture.

"I was raised on a small farm in Kent. We were a stone's throw from the seaside," he told her mother. "My parents both still live there and raise animals for sale as well as making money in the fishing trade."

Sebastian raised his eyebrows. "I was raised on a farm in Yorkshire, myself. It is honest work, I'd wager your parents were very proud of you," he commended as he started pouring wine for everyone.

Captain Aubrey nodded almost bashfully as he accepted his glass of wine. "Yes, they are."

"Do you visit them very often?" Little J asked innocently. Kitty smiled as her sister got involved in the conversation, anymore sulking and it would be obvious that she hadn't planned on actually spending her day in Hyde Park.

"I try, but I don't often succeed. It is very rare that we have an extended period of time to travel to see our families. I make it out for Christmas every now and then, but they understand. It would be easier if I was just a naval officer but as I am Captain I have other responsibilities."

"Understandable," Sebastian nodded. "Do you have siblings that aid your parents?"

Captain Aubrey shook his head. "No, they were not blessed after me."

"It happens, son," Sebastian said sympathetically. "My parents had no further children after my only sister and Em and I haven't any more since Henry."

Emilia blushed bright red as she glared at Sebastian. Kitty muffled a laugh as she knew her mother was sensitive to discuss such personal matters. "I think everyone is hungry!" she exclaimed as she motioned for everyone to eat.

Kitty couldn't hold her giggle in any longer and every joined in.

When mid afternoon became late afternoon Sebastian initiated their return to Ethridge. Kitty found herself walking beside Captain Aubrey again, though not on purpose. She noticed that he seemed to be the one orchestrating that.

"Will you be sad when you depart at the end of the week, Captain?" Kitty asked nervously. She didn't want there to be a lull in conversation.

"I do enjoy the sea, Lady Kitty, but I do miss the people back on land. I can tell you that months on end with only men can be quite dull," he laughed.

Kitty giggled as well. "I can imagine," she agreed. "What is the likelihood that you will encounter pirates on your journey?" she asked him after a moment.

Captain Aubrey pursed his lips. "The route we are taking is a dangerous one, and it is notorious for all sorts of marauders, Lady Kitty, but it is what we have been trained for," he assured her. "We're just to escort a few cargo ships safely and then we'll return for our next assignment. Hopefully it will be somewhere in British waters so that I might have a chance to see a few familiar faces before we set off for India or somewhere like that."

"India?" Kitty raised her eyebrows, impressed. "What is India like?"

"India is very warm, but the people are fascinating. They have a whole other belief system to us, they don't share our God, but it is captivating to experience their culture. I can tell you though that I can do without the food, it is a little too spicy for my liking. But I would be honoured to return one day," he told her, remembering fondly.

Kitty wished she had been to faraway places. She hadn't been anywhere on a ship. Her father hadn't allowed the family to travel to France because of all the political uprising and he didn't trust the security of oceanic travel because of the risk of pirate attacks. The furthest she had been was Scotland for a time staying at a house that overlooked one of their lovely lochs.

"Would you ever retire from the navy?" Kitty wondered aloud. "To marry and start a family?" She immediately regretted asking the question. It was too obvious, and she lacked the ability to sound blasé.

"To be honest I'd never really thought about it. I suppose if I met the right woman then I would. I've always wanted to live by the sea … as you know I love it. I think it would be an idyllic place to raise a family, don't you think?"

Kitty nodded. "I find the seaside quite calming," she agreed. "Well I hope you meet her," she smiled.

"Meet who?" he furrowed his eyebrows.

"Your wife," she prompted.

"Oh, yes, as do I," he smiled. "Lady Kitty, I do find your conversation very enthralling. I'm glad there is no malice between us. I do hope I can consider you a friend from now on."

Kitty beamed. "I am glad my conversation is now 'enthralling' as you say. Not too long ago I was 'ridiculous.'"

Captain Aubrey nodded guiltily.

Once they'd arrived back at Ethridge the women departed to their bedchambers followed by a maid to help them get ready for the dinner party at Lady Russel's. Kitty liked Lady Russel. She was an older lady, older than her parents, and a widow, so she enjoyed a handsome income thanks to her late husband.

Kitty was helped into a clean chemise by one of the maids, Flora. Flora then tightened Kitty's corset around her waist so that she had the perfect hourglass figure. Most women by the time they come of the age to start wearing a corset had trained themselves to take shallow breaths. Kitty was an expert.

"Breath in, milady," Flora instructed and Kitty did just that as she pulled the drawstrings once more.

Kitty clutched her sides as the corset narrowed her waist. "Why must women wear these things?" she complained.

"Men don't. They let their stomaches hang out and nobody judges them for it."

Flora sighed. "I know, milady, but we are women, and they are men. If they like girls with little waists then that's what they'll have. I don't make the rules, I just follow them."

Kitty rolled her eyes. "It is a stupid rule."

"I know," Flora laughed lightly. "Now, have you selected a gown for this evening?"

Once Kitty's corset was properly laced she went over to her wardrobe and pulled out a deep blue gown. She'd chosen the fabric especially as it had matched her eyes. Her mother had commissioned it for her birthday and she hadn't found the right opportunity to wear it until then. The gown was the latest fashion, with the sleeves completely off the shoulders. All that held the dress up was a gathered material sleeve around the upper arm. The bodice was tight to the body and had been embroidered with thread the same shade of blue as the material to add subtle texture. The skirt flared down to the ground from the hips in yards of smooth satin.

"That's lovely," Flora gushed.

Kitty smiled as she nodded. "I know it is. It is the loveliest dress I own."

"Are you trying to impress anyone?" Flora asked curiously.

Kitty's eyes snapped up from the dress to the young maid. "Flora, all I need is for you to help me into my dress," she snapped angrily. She wasn't dressing to impress anyone; she was only trying to look nice.

"I apologise, milady," Flora said bashfully as she took the dress from Kitty to unbutton the back so that Kitty could step into it.

"Don't worry Flora," Kitty replied. "I'm sorry for being short; I just want to be ready."

Within the hour Flora had finished twisting and pinning Kitty's hair and she was finally ready. She couldn't help but think, as Flora was decorating her hair, back to the conversation she had had with Captain Aubrey about the fact that he liked her hair out and natural. As she exited her bedchamber she met Little J who had just been experiencing the same treatment. Her golden coloured locks were pinned in a similar fashion to hers and her soft yellow coloured dress brought out the lovely light tints in her hair.

"Kitty, you look marvellous," Little J beamed as she surveyed her sister.

"Thank you, Little J, as do you. It is odd to see you dressed so finely ... or course that is because you are hardly ever in attendance of one of the functions we are asked to as you are at church," Kitty teased.

Little J rolled her eyes. "Don't say such things around mama and papa, alright?" she pleaded.

Kitty looped her arm around Little J's elbow. "Whatever secret you're keeping is safe with me," she promised.

When the two sisters arrived downstairs the carriages were already waiting. The first already contained her parents, Sabine and her two younger brothers which meant that the last carriage was for Little J, Captain Aubrey and herself.

As they stepped outside Kitty suddenly wished she'd donned a travelling coat as there was a chill in the air, almost as if it were to pour down with rain at any moment, but it was already dusk and she didn't have time to return upstairs to find something warmer to wear.

Captain Aubrey appeared beside the carriage to help the two young ladies into the carriage. He was once again dressed in his naval uniform but this time with all is lovely decorations. Her favourite, she decided, was the beautiful gold hilted sword that she wore on his side.

"You look absolutely beautiful, ladies," he smiled as he helped them both into the carriage. "Beautiful," he repeated softly as Kitty let go of his hand and took her seat beside her younger sister.

Kitty blushed slightly and was glad that the carriage was not brightly illuminated. Once Captain Aubrey had taken his seat opposite them and the footmen had closed the door, both carriages took off.

"Is Lady Russel's residence very far?" Captain Aubrey asked.

Little J shook her head. "That's the beauty of London, getting around is not too hard."

"What generally happens at dinner parties?" he asked next. "I've never actually attended one. This is my first stationing in London and it is all pretty foreign to me."

"There are usually around five courses, more depending on the host. Then and informal gathering where they serve tea and cakes and then someone will play the pianoforte and sing for us. Lady Russel is never biased in her choice for who she selects. Though Little J is a favourite, she excels in anything that requires learning," Kitty nudged her little sister.

"I am a partisan of education," she said exasperatedly. "I know it's ridiculous because I am a woman but I'm not going to let information just sit there when I can learn it."

Kitty giggled. "Don't worry, Little J, we still love you."

"I think it is commendable," Captain Aubrey said casually. "If anyone had the aptitude for learning and they do not pursue it then that is a crime in my eyes. It is a shame that you are female, milady. I do not mean that in a demeaning way it is just a fact."

Little J nodded. "I know, trust me," she sighed.

Kitty suddenly felt nervous as they arrived at Lady Russel's. Sir Walter would be there, and all eyes would be on her as she began to change her ways. She just hoped that the change would be good.

Chapter 6

"Oh, welcome, welcome!" exclaimed Lady Russel as the Alcott family and their guests entered her humble abode. "I'm so pleased you could make it, Lord and Lady Ethridge, I fear at those large balls we hardly ever get to have a proper conversation!" Lady Russel led them through her house directly into her formal dining room. It was decorated beautifully with large bouquets of flowers spaced evenly along the long, rectangular mahogany table.

Kitty was impressed, everything looked divine. It looked like her family were the last to arrive. A few small groups of people were standing around talking quietly, including Sir Walter Martin.

Lady Russel cleared her throat to get everyone's attention. She looked lovely that evening. Her brilliant red hair was smooth and elegant in a neat knot and her emerald gown perfectly matched her green eyes. "If everyone would like to take their seats, we'll have the first course." Lady Russel motioned for the footmen to pull the chairs out for her guests.

Kitty felt slightly uncomfortable when she found that she was seated beside Sir Walter. She knew what she had to do, but she felt that she would have a little more time to rehearse what she had to say. She was sitting nowhere near Captain Aubrey much to her disappointment; he was down the other end of the table with her parents and Lady Russel. Sitting next to her was Sabine and then Little J.

Kitty stole a glance at Sir Walter who was wearing a rather solemn look on his rounded face. His black hair was, like always, slicked back, and his short bead was combed neatly. "How are you this evening, Sir Walter?" she asked quietly as a small bowl of water cress soup was placed before her by one of the footmen.

Sir Walter's sharp, grey eyes flashed to her. "Perfectly fine, Lady Kitty," he snapped quietly.

Kitty knew that he was very angry with her. She figured she would just have to give her apology without rehearsal. "Sir Walter, I wanted to apologise to you for my behaviour, it was inexcusable the way I treated you. You didn't deserve that," she said softly as she placed a small spoonful of soup in her mouth.

"No, I didn't," he replied curtly. "But I should've known better than to think that a silly little twit, like yourself, was ever good enough for a man as accomplished as I am."

Kitty's eyes widened in astonishment. Had he really just said that her? "I should advise you to hold your tongue when you insult me, sir; I am the eldest daughter of a very fine gentleman."

"I'm sure that very fine gentleman would abandon you quite quickly if he knew that he had bred a little slut," he hissed under his breath so that no one around would hear.

Kitty checked her surroundings and was glad to see that Sabine and Little J were deep in conversation so they had not heard what Sir Walter had sad about her. She then looked down at the green soup before her and suddenly didn't feel so hungry anymore.

"There is no need to be unkind, Sir Walter, I am trying to do the right thing by apologising to you," Kitty said softly. She willed herself not to cry. She could feel the tears wanting to escape her eyelids but she wouldn't let them.

"The right thing to do would to have not been entertaining me with false insinuations that you were interested in knowing me better, Lady Kitty," Sir Walter replied quietly. "I am a gentleman and a fine match for a worthy young woman; you are a harlot who is no better than the prostitutes on the streets."

Kitty didn't reply to him. Was he right? Sir Walter was not the first man she had teased. Did they all think of her so darkly? She did her best to eat the soup any by the time the next course of escargot was served she had consumed perhaps half of it.

"Kitty, are you alright?" Sabine whispered to her.

Kitty looked to her cousin and suddenly realised that most people had nearly finished their second course and she hadn't even touched hers. How much time had passed? She put on a false smile and nodded. "Quite alright," she assured her. "I was just admiring the general splendour that I forgot to eat."

Sabine smiled, satisfied with her answer. "Well, try them, they really are delicious, though do not tell Cook in Southerby, for she will be heartbroken that I prefer another's French cuisine to her own."

Kitty laughed to make sure she was convinced of her good mood. "Your secret is safe with me," she promised.

For the remainder of the meal she made small talk with those sitting opposite her on the table and with her sister and cousin. She did everything in her power not to look in Sir Walter's direction for fear of a flood of tears that would surely come.

Once the meal was over Lady Russel suggested that they all retire to the drawing room so that a young lady could delight them all on the pianoforte. She also ordered the footmen for wine, fruit and cheese to be served promptly.

As soon as everyone had risen from their seats, Captain Aubrey was beside her. "What did he say that upset you so?" he asked quietly, his voice still thick with concern.

Kitty shook her head without meeting his eyes. "Nothing," she lied. "Absolutely nothing."

Lady Russel's drawing room had been especially re-arranged for her function that evening. The sofas had been repositioned to face the lovely white pianoforte and extra chairs had been added so that everyone would have a seat.

"Lady Jane," Lady Russel called out as soon as everyone had gathered in the drawing room. "Little J, dear, will you please delight us with your skills?" she asked, gesturing to the pianoforte.

Little J pursed her lips and nodded. Kitty knew that her sister hated singing and performing, but it didn't make her any worse at it. She was exceptionally talented. Kitty quickly occupied a single chair in the back so that nobody could sit beside her.

Little J had memorised many pieces, her favourite being the works by Franz Schubert. Kitty knew what she was to play before Little J had even taken her seat before the pianoforte. She was to play "Ellens dritter Gesang" or "Ellen's Third Song". Kitty liked Schubert very much. Little J liked his music not only because it was beautiful but because it didn't require her to sing.

As Little J began to play to beautifully all eyes were on her. Everyone was smiling peacefully as the footmen entered bearing platters of food as well as a decanter filled with wine.

The music allowed Kitty to think deeply about what Sir Walter had said about her. She had done the right thing by apologising, and it was a genuine apology. She now knew that her behavior had consequences and she was doing her best to better herself. But what if everyone she had ever teased thought she was no better than a prostitute? She'd never given herself to a man, she'd never even kissed a man before, she was definitely better than a prostitute.

She didn't realise that she had been crying until she tasted her tears on her lips. She rose from her chair quietly and crept out of the drawing room hoping to appear unnoticed. She didn't have a handkerchief on her so she would have to search for one. She wasn't familiar with the halls of Lady Russel's house so she was guessing where she was walking. She came to a long hallway that was highlighted by a large gilded mirror in the centre of the wall. She stood before it and surveyed her face. It was obvious that she had been crying as her eyelids were very red. She wiped all of the remaining tears away and then fanned her face with her hands.

"Pull yourself together, Kitty," she told herself. She straightened the skirt of her gown self consciously and adjusted the sleeves on her arms before turning back towards the direction of the drawing room. She hoped that her eyes returned to normal before she had to converse with anyone.

As she turned she jumped as she realised there was in fact a person standing not five yards from her. He was standing just outside the mirror reflection so that she hadn't seen him.

"Sir Walter," she gasped. "What are you doing?"

Sir Walter took a deep breath as he glared at her. "You always manage to get what you want, no matter whom you squash in the process," he said bitterly. He walked closer to her so that their bodies were about ten inches apart.

Kitty's heart beat picked up as his steel grey eyes burned into her. She had nowhere to step back as all that was behind her was the gilded mirror. She wanted to be back in the drawing room where her family was, she wanted to be where she felt safe. Standing there with Sir Walter was not safe.

"Believe me, Sir Walter, I do not squash intentionally," she whispered nervously.

His was twice her height and width and was ever so slightly closing the distance between him. He no longer looked angry, he looked lustful.

Kitty knew this was how girls were ruined, but she did not want it to be against her will. "Sir Walter, I'd like you to move away from my person, please," she said firmly, trying to sound brave.

A smile spread across his face as she spoke. "I told my mother about you, you know," he informed her giddily. "I told her that the most beautiful young woman was allowing me to pursue her. I couldn't believe that someone so lovely fancied me. And then you showed your true colours. They turned out to be very dirty. You're not clean enough to introduce to my mother. You're clean enough for an abandoned corridor though."

As he spoke that last sentence his hands were on her waist pulling her to him. Their mouths collided and Kitty's screams were muffled by his force. His hands covered her body quickly, one secured in her hair holding her face to his and the other on her backside, gathering up her skirts. She made her hands into fists and did her best to punch Sir Walter to get him off of her.

Kitty used all the strength she had not to open her mouth when she felt his tongue on her lips. She screamed as loud as she could but Sir Walter made it impossible for any sound to come out.

Her tears saturated her face as she was about to stop fighting. She wasn't strong enough to stop fighting. As she let her hands drop to her side Sir Walter disappeared. Her legs gave way as her skirt returned back down to the floor. Violent sobs caused her body to shake, but through the tears she could see the shine of a silver blade at Sir Walter's throat.

"You dare lay a hand on an unwilling woman?" Captain Aubrey spat.

"She wasn't unwilling," replied a humoured Sir Walter.

"Do not insult my intelligence," he seethed. "It is taking everything I have not to flick my wrist and have my sword take out your throat."

As Kitty's tears cleared the figures before her were no longer blurred. She could hear voices coming down the corridor, but the alarmed voice of her mother stood out over all. "What is going on?" she cried. "Kitty, what are you doing on the floor?"

Her mother's arms enveloped her as the men surrounded Captain Aubrey and Sir Walter.

"What is happening?" she heard her father ask. "Sir Walter ... Captain, what had happened?"

"Lord Ethridge, this man just attempted to rape your daughter," Captain Aubrey hissed.

Emilia let out a pained cry as she held Kitty tighter and Sebastian lunged for Captain Aubrey's sword. It all happened very quickly from Kitty's perspective. Her father was trying to kill Sir Walter as both her brother's tried to hold their father back. Captain Aubrey was doing his best to hold off her father as well as keep Sir Walter at bay. Several other guests surrounded them so Sir Walter couldn't get away.

Kitty wanted it to be over, she wanted to be out of there. She didn't want to ever have this incident mentioned again. But she knew that London society would never let that happen, she would be the subject of gossip until someone became pregnant out of wedlock.

"I'll send for the police," Lady Russel exclaimed. "Do not do anything you will regret!"

Kitty knew that Lady Russel was talking to her father. He had stopped going for Captain Aubrey's sword but he was still shaking with pure fury.

"Lady Russel is right, Lord Ethridge, you're needed here more than you are in jail. Jail is where this man will rot," Captain Aubrey seethed.

Sebastian turned away from Sir Walter and Captain Aubrey toward Kitty and Emilia who were on the floor still. "Come on, darling, I'm getting you out of here." He knelt down on the ground and looped his arms behind her knees and around her back and lifted her off of the ground.

Kitty closed her eyes as she laid her head against her father's chest. She felt safe in his arms, a feeling that she knew would feel foreign to her in many situations from then on. She could hear her mother following them swiftly.

"I won't let anyone hurt you ever again, Kitty," he promised her as he carried her to the foyer of Lady Russel's house. "That man will hang if I have anything to do with it." She heard him call for Little J and Sabine who were in the nearby drawing room to follow him outside to the carriage.

As they rode her father informed them of what had occurred in the corridor with Sir Walter, and like him they were all outraged.

Kitty didn't open her eyes until the carriage pulled up outside her house. She just wanted to be alone with her thoughts. Once the women were all out of the carriage her father returned to Lady Russel's to make sure that Sir Walter had been arrested. Kitty knew that if he received a punishment it would not be hard; the law was not fair to females.

Kitty was grateful to her family when they left her be out in the courtyard that she had visited a few times that week. It was well into the night and the stars were very prominent in the sky. It soothed her, so she could see why Captain Aubrey liked it so much.

She sat down on the stone floor and hugged her knees tightly. At that point she didn't care if her best gown was ruined, it was tainted anyway.

"The police arrested Sir Walter, though there isn't much they can do, they say, as nothing actually happened. He can plead his innocence quite easily. I now wish that I'd cut his throat," Captain Aubrey informed her.

Kitty jumped at the sudden presence of another. She had no idea how long she had been sitting on the floor but she felt the chill from the stone quite immensely. "I knew he would get away with it. He is a gentleman and I'm just a silly woman," Kitty replied solemnly. "Anyway, if you'd killed him then you would be the one hanging."

"It would have been worth it," he replied seriously as he sat down beside her. Kitty saw that his appearance was no longer so crisp. His dark blond hair was untidy and his naval coat was undone. "There is a special place in hell for men who touch women against their will."

Kitty hoped that was true. "He called me dirty," she said quietly. "He said that I wasn't clean enough ... I'm inclined to believe it."

Captain Aubrey took her hand and squeezed it reassuringly. What Kitty liked was the fact that she didn't mind the contact. He had saved her from Sir Walter, he was a protector. "That man ... he's not even a man; he belongs with the rodents in the sewers. He is evil in every sense of the word. You are not dirty, you are pure and beautiful."

Kitty smiled slightly at him. "Thank you for saving me. It seems all you've done in London is save me."

Captain Aubrey's face crinkled as he smiled broadly. "Happy to be of service, ma'am," he said, pretending to tip his hat. "I don't know what I would have done if I had got there too late," he said shaking his head. "I would not have been able to stop myself from killing him."

"How did you find me? I wandered off trying to find a handkerchief and I ended up in the corridor."

"I've told you before that I'm good at observing. I saw you leave and then I saw Sir Walter follow you. There was something about him that I didn't trust and I'm glad I followed my instincts," he replied. Kitty liked the fact that he was still holding her hand, it was comforting.

"I'm glad you did too," Kitty sighed. "I'm not angry at Sir Walter for the obvious reason, I'm glad that his true nature has been discovered so that he won't be left alone with any other young girl ... and hopefully he will be expelled from several social circles ... but I'm angry at him because ..." Kitty suddenly regretted starting the sentence. It was embarrassing to tell Captain Aubrey of all people what she was angry at Sir Walter for.

"Because what?" he pressed.

Kitty groaned and hung her head. "Because he stole my first ... kiss," she whispered, barely audible.

"Your first kiss?" Captain Aubrey raised his eyebrows. "I don't think that that can be considered your first kiss, Lady Kitty."

Kitty nodded. "I just imagined my first kiss being with someone that I loved."

"It will be, the next time you kiss someone, you will love them and they will love you, I promise you that," he said sincerely.

"How can you know that, Captain Aubrey?" Kitty asked, raising her eyebrows.

"I just do," he smiled coyly. "And please, you are not one of my men, call me 'William.'"

Chapter 7

One would assume that after the ordeal that Kitty had experienced the night before at Lady Russel's that she would have been anxious and frightened to venture out into the world, but she wasn't. He calmed her, Captain Aubrey, he quashed her fears. She was sure of her previous thoughts ... he was a protector.

He cared for people, like no other she knew. He was not related to her which meant that he had no obligation to defend her but he still did. He worried himself about others and that was a very attractive quality in a person.

She was awoken the next morning by her younger sister climbing into bed with her. Kitty liked it when Little J joined her in bed in the morning. They didn't spend much time together as there wasn't much opportunity. They were no longer children so they couldn't go down to the pond whenever they wanted. They were out in society and therefore there were certain expectations.

Kitty rolled over to see Little J lying next to her peacefully. She was smiling sympathetically, obviously trying to be empathetic.

"How are you this morning, Kitty?" she whispered softly.

Kitty smiled and shrugged her shoulders as best she could whilst lying horizontally. "I'm alright," she said truthfully. "Nothing happened, Captain Aubrey saw to that."

Little J's blue eyes sparkled. "I know," she gushed. "It was so heroic. I was very impressed ... I wonder what it would be like to have a man defend my honour."

Kitty rolled her eyes. "I will agree that it was heroic, but he was not defending my honour. The man was vile; he was doing the right thing." She was not going to reveal to her sister that Captain Aubrey had made her feel safer than she had ever felt before. That was a thought she wanted to keep private. If Little J could have secrets then so could she.

Little J shuffled over to her on the bed and kissed her cheek. "Think what you want, you and I both know what happened. I'm so glad you're safe and home with us. I don't know what I would have done if he'd hurt you."

When undressing the night before Kitty had seen that she had purple bruises on her legs and waist but it wasn't bad. She wasn't about to worry her family with them. They would go away eventually.

"You needn't fret about me, Little J, I'm stronger than I look," Kitty smiled at her little sister. Truth be told, Kitty didn't know what she would have done if Captain Aubrey hadn't come when he did. If he hadn't she could have well been pregnant with his bastard child ... or worse, dead.

"I don't doubt it, Kitty. You were always the most outgoing out of the three girls. I don't think you could even put 'outgoing' and 'Annie' in the same sentence," she giggled.

"That reminds me, it's Sunday," Kitty sighed. "I wish we didn't have to go to church. Dressing up and listening to sermons for hours really puts me to sleep, even if it is Annie's husband."

"He's passionate," Little J said encouragingly. "I commend him for following his love. He is lucky that he is able to do what he loves - preaching. I cannot do what I love," she said sadly.

Kitty arched one of her eyebrows. "And what is it exactly that you love doing?"

Little J blushed and sat up in Kitty's bed. "Obeying the rules," she lied obviously.

Kitty shook her head, sitting up as well. "You will tell me, won't you?"

Little J nodded. "Eventually," she promised. "Just not yet, I can't just yet."

Kitty accepted it. "Alright," she sighed. "Let us rise before mama sends up a search party. Sunday is always such a production."

"Mama won't expect you to attend church, especially to-day. I could go downstairs and ask her if you're allowed to lie in," Little J offered.

Kitty shook her head. "If I do not appear those who have already gossiped will expect that I am ashamed of something, I'm sure Sir Walter has already labelled me a seductress to those who will believe his lies. I won't cower."

Little J appeared murderous. "Papa will set the misinformed straight, I promise you that. The law may not be fair to females, Kitty, but we do have men on our side that will fight for us."

Kitty smiled gratefully at her sister as she rose from bed as well. She slipped into her wrap and fastened it at her waist. "Sometimes I dream of a time when women and men will be equal. Wouldn't that be grand? We could own land and vote and attend university," Kitty thought wildly. "But it is ridiculous, isn't it? We live in a world of ignorance."

Little J nodded. "I feel the exact same way. It will never happen though, men rule the world, and while men rule there will be no rights for women."

Kitty shook her head. "No, I disagree. There are some men that listen to what women have to say. Like papa, he listen's too all of us and lets us make our own decisions. It is little steps like that that bring us closer."

"I hope you're right. I would like to see my children one day attending university if they wish," Little J sighed. She ran her fingers through her untidy blonde hair and tried to untangle the knots. "I suppose I'd better go and dress ready for church. Do you want me to help you or send for one of the maids?"

Kitty shook her head, not wanting any of the maids to see her bruises. "No, I'll be alright by myself, don't you worry," she smiled at Little J.

Little J departed her bedchamber and Kitty immediately went over to her wardrobe to find a gown that she could wear that did not require assistance to put on. As she examined each gown she was angered to find that so many had buttons all the way down the back. She found one ivory coloured gown that had a corset - like back. She could feasibly tie the gown up herself.

She laid the gown out on the bed along with its matching bonnet and parasol as well as a few baubles to accompany the outfit. She then placed a few coins into a purse to give to the church upon their exit.

She slipped into a freshly laundered chemise and then stepped into her corset, bringing it up around her torso. As soon as the weight of the corset touched her bruises she winced in pain. There was no way that she would be able to sit in church for hours with that pressure on her bruises. She stepped out of the corset and looked at her figure in the mirror. She wasn't as thin as she was with the corset but her waist was still narrow. She smiled at the idea of walking into the House of God being improperly dressed - how scandalous. If anyone knew they would truly think she was a seductress.

As she stepped into her gown she remembered the sight of Captain Aubrey holding his sword to Sir Walter's throat. She felt safe knowing that he was in her house. She felt safe so long as he always had an eye on her. How would she feel when he shipped out in five days? She could imagine feeling more vulnerable than ever. What if she saw Sir Walter and Captain Aubrey was in the middle of the ocean?

Her mind immediately flashed to the moment right before Sir Walter touched her. Feeling absolutely terrified of what she knew was about to happen and the fact that she was completely defenceless.

She had changed her behaviour for the better; perhaps she would be able to change her strength too.

Kitty didn't fuss over her hair, just pinning it up into a simple knot before putting her bonnet on her head and tying the ribbon into a bow under her chin.

When she finally arrived downstairs after retrieving her bible from the table beside her bed she found that only her father and brothers were there sitting in the dining room having a cup of tea wearing their Sunday best. Breakfast on a Sunday was never a formal affair in the Alcott house. There was usually on a cup of tea and perhaps a boiled egg before they left for church.

They immediately stood and looked at her sympathetically. Her father especially looked saddened. "Kitty, darling, come sit by me," he offered, gesturing to the seat that belonged to her mother.

Kitty smiled slightly and shook her head. "No, that's quite alright," she refused politely, taking her usual seat. One of the footmen placed a china teacup before her and filled it with lovely smelling tea. "Thank you," she said gratefully and she poured in some milk and stirred in a sugar cube.

"How are you this morning, Kit?" Henry asked her cautiously.

Kitty turned to her younger brother. She didn't have an opportunity to speak with Henry much as he was always away at school. And even when he was home on breaks he was often spending time with James or their parents. It was comforting to know that he cared. "I'm fine, nothing happened, so I'm alright."

"The bloody police are useless," Sebastian growled. Kitty was not alarmed at his profanity; he did have a right to be upset.

"Papa, it isn't the police, it is the law. They don't make the law, they just enforce it," Kitty replied quietly.

"Nevertheless, I won't hear of my daughter's going anywhere without a chaperone from now on," he said firmly. "We all thought of Sir Walter as a gentleman and how wrong we were. It goes for Little J as well; she will no longer be going to the park or travelling to Annie's on her own. She will have a chaperone with her at all times."

Kitty knew it was the right thing to have a chaperone with her, for her safety as well as for propriety. But she knew that Little J wouldn't like that.

"Papa, surely a trip to the park or to Annie's isn't dangerous," James protested. "Little J knows how to look after herself."

Kitty stared her brother. She knew he was saying those things because he wanted Little J's freedom but did he really think that she was not capable of taking care of herself?

"I do hope that when you are a father, James, that you will not see your daughter violated by such a man. There will be chaperones in this house and I will not be argued with," he snapped at his eldest son. He turned to Kitty and sighed. "How are you, darling, truthfully?"

"Papa, I know I'm safe with everyone here looking out for me." Kitty broke the shell of a boiled egg with a spoon and salted its contents while she waited for everyone to arrive downstairs.

"I think that our family will refrain from attending too many gatherings from here on out," Sebastian sighed. "You, my dear, are not that interested in finding a husband ... come to think of it neither Little J nor Sabine are either. I think it would be prudent to have some familial time before Henry goes back to Eton and James starts back his lessons at Oxford. We shall have Annie and Joseph to dinner more often and have a few more afternoons like we did the other day in the park. I miss having all five of you at home."

Kitty liked the idea of that. Suddenly frivolity and laughter at balls seemed pointless. Her behaviour had led Sir Walter to think that he had every right to lay his hands on her like she was some common girl at a brothel. Sir Walter was one of many who had fancied themselves popular with her so it was only a matter of time before another man cornered her. Familial time was definitely in order.

One by one her family members arrived downstairs dressed in their conservative finery. Her mother, by far, stood out in her pale green gown that emphasised her flawless hourglass figure. She never ceased to amaze Kitty with her effortless beauty. Kitty hoped that she aged as well as her mother, even if she had inherited her paternal family's eyes and hair colour.

"Ah, Em," her father beamed. "I was just telling Kitty, James and Henry that I've decided that we shall withdraw a bit from the social season. We'll spend more time together as a family. Also, the girls are not allowed anywhere without a chaperone, there will be no exceptions on that."

Immediately after Sebastian had said that, Little J's jaw dropped. "But papa!" she protested.

"Little J, what did I just say?" he sighed exasperatedly. "Chaperones, no arguments," he said slowly. "Any excursions that you take you will be accompanied by a sister, a brother, a parent, or a maid, do I make myself clear?"

Little J pursed her lips and nodded. "Crystal," she murmured. Kitty could tell ideas were flying around in her head of how to elude a chaperone.

"I think it's a wonderful idea," Emilia said happily. "We need to spend some more time together. Before you know it, Kitty will be off and married to some duke who will probably live God knows where, Little J -" but before she could finish she was interrupted by Captain Aubrey entering the dining room looking a little out of breath.

"Pardon me, my Lady, but did you say Kitty was getting married?" he asked curiously. His bright blue eyes found her immediately. He looked a little alarmed.

Emilia laughed lightly. "No, I don't think that will ever happen," she dismissed it. "It was pure imagination. Since our plans between you were quite ridiculous we've given up, haven't we Sebastian?" Emilia turned to her husband who nodded.

Kitty felt mortified. Her parents were openly discussing their plans for a union between her and Captain Aubrey when they were standing in the same room. A union between herself and Captain Aubrey was utterly ridiculous. For starters he was never in England except for when he had leave, and even then the navy had been stationed in London for a matter of weeks and they were already leaving. He didn't a title and he was not a gentleman ... but he did have a fortune, and that was what a lady of her stature looked for in a man. It was encouraged by many that young ladies accept advantageous proposals that offered power and position, but Kitty wasn't bothered by those sorts of things anymore.

Simply marrying for a title and a living was not what she wanted any longer. She wanted someone who made her feel safe and secure. She wanted someone who loved only her and didn't feel the need to bed other women. She wanted someone who was brave and loyal and would drop anything for her. She wanted a protector.

She was snapped out of her trance when her father spoke his name. "I don't believe I've thanked you, Captain Aubrey, for your services to my family last night. I will be forever indebted to you. Anything we can do for you, please ask, anything."

"It was my duty, milord, anyone would have done it," Captain Aubrey said bashfully.

"No, they wouldn't," Emilia said firmly. "You protected her, and we thank you for it," she smiled warmly.

Kitty heard the word again, the one that she had thought so many times - protect. He was opinionated and he knew what he wanted in a woman - he made that clear when he pointed out every single flaw Kitty possessed - but he was chivalrous and noble and he cared about people. One didn't find that in a man very often.

His eyes were on her as he spoke. "I'm glad I was there," he said, and Kitty knew he was speaking to her instead of the whole room. "I don't know what I would have done if Lady Kitty had been harmed."

Kitty knew exactly what he would have done, and she was sure that seeing him hanging by the neck until dead was not how she wanted to see her saviour.

"Nor I," he father said angrily. "Come along then, we haven't time for any breakfast, we're already behind schedule. Joseph will be starting his sermon in thirty minutes," he said as he began ushering them all out of the dining room.

Once again Captain Aubrey waited for her before walking out of the dining room. "How are you this morning?" he asked tenderly.

"I've a feeling that I will need to write 'fine' on my forehead so I won't have to answer that question any longer," Kitty grinned to which he laughed heartily.

"You are fine though?" he asked once he'd finished laughing.

Kitty nodded. "The way I see it, it could have been worse. The fact of the matter is that nothing happened." As she spoke those words she subconsciously brushed her hand over the bruises on her waist. It felt strange not to feel the bones of her corset.

"Does your family always refer to the reverend by his Christian name?" he asked curiously as they walked outside to where the carriages were waiting for them.

Kitty nodded. "We do when he is our brother - in - law, my youngest sister, Annie, is married to him."

He furrowed his eyebrows, confused. "Your father allowed his daughter to marry a man of the cloth?"

Kitty nodded. "My father is not a monster; if his child is in love then he will allow the marriage. He grew up leanly so he knows how genuine less fortunate people are."

"I would have thought that he would want titles for his daughters. I certainly don't have one which is why I was surprised a union was insinuated between us."

"I suppose many earls would want titles for their daughters," Kitty granted him that. The carriage door was opened for her by one of the footmen. Her sister and Sabine climbed in first and she was to follow. "But what is a title when one could have love?" she asked him and then turned to climb into the carriage. The door was closed behind her as they were sitting in the smaller carriage, the phaeton. They rest of the family would follow in the larger carriage. Kitty was glad that Captain Aubrey would not be joining them, for she was sure she would blush in his presence.

Chapter 8

It wasn't that long before they arrived at their church. The congregation was gathered outside before Reverend Preston would admit them. The church was a lovely white building with gorgeous stone steps leading up to the main building. From the skies it looked like a cross so that when God looked down he would know it was a holy building … or so Kitty had been told.

Kitty spotted her youngest sister chatting with a few of the other ladies animatedly. To see Annie being so social made Kitty and the rest of her family know that Joseph was perfect for her. Before him she was so shy and introverted, and now she enjoyed striking up conversations with people and being her delightful charming self around those that she had previously shied away from.

The driver helped the three young ladies from the carriage and they all made a beeline for the smiling Annie. Since marrying she had dressed a little more conservatively, especially as she was the reverend's wife, but she was still just as little and lovely as ever. Annie was the image of their mother. Her hair was the exact shade of gold and her eyes were a delicious chocolate brown. She had the same shaped figure as Emilia which Kitty was envious of. She wished she was voluptuous like her sister and her mother but she wasn't at all.

As they walked through the crowd of people, Kitty could feel eyes on her, questioning eyes. She was both marvelled and disgusted by how fast gossip travelled in London.

"Annie!" Little J exclaimed as they neared her. They caught their sister's attention and she immediately excused herself from her conversation.

Annie beamed at her sisters and her cousin as she came over and hugged every one of them. She was wearing a soft, black gown with feminine lace trim as well as a matching bonnet. A few wayward tendrils hung beneath her bonnet but for the most part her blonde hair was pinned up.

"I was beginning to think that you wouldn't come!" Annie exclaimed. "I read over Joseph's sermon this morning and it is anything but dull. I truly think you'll all find it invigorating!"

Kitty rolled her eyes. "Darling, even the word sermon sounds dull. I just wish I had a pillow so that I could get some extra sleep."

Annie smirked at her elder sister. "I know even you will love this one. Please be kind, he puts so much effort in every week – it's not that simple to make religion entertaining you know."

Kitty smiled and hugged Annie again. "I know it isn't," she conceded. "I've missed you, Annie, you've been spending all your time with Little J and none with me," Kitty complained just to unnerve Little J.

Annie's brown eyes widened as she turned to Little J. "How many times have we seen each other this week, Little J?" she asked her sister. Kitty knew Annie didn't know what Little J was up to, but she was covering for her as she was a good sister.

"I think about four," Little J recalled.

Sabine giggled. "Seriously, the secrets you all have. My mama would have found this out by now ... but perhaps it is because you cannot hide anything in my house with two younger brothers."

"No, it is because you are too pure of heart, Sabine. You cannot lie and that is a very attractive trait in a young woman," Kitty informed her elder cousin.

Sabine rolled her blue eyes and smiled coyly.

"I'm not lying," Little J protested. "I'm just withholding some information about my daily schedule that is not imperative for you to know."

Annie's eyes brightened up suddenly. "Mama!" she exclaimed as she walked over to hug Emilia.

The three other girls turned to see the rest of the Alcott party arriving at the church.

"Hello, darling," Emilia smiled as she wrapped her arms tightly around her youngest daughter. "A week really is too long to not see each other. You and Joseph must come to Ethridge at least three times this week for dinner, I insist."

Annie laughed lightly. "Alright, mama, I'm sure we'll be glad to," she accepted.

The doors to the church opened and Annie's husband, the reverend, began ushering his congregation inside. Kitty had always thought that Joseph was handsome in a subtle kind of way. His hair was a dirty blond colour and his eyes were a brilliant green. He had a nice straight nose and an angular jaw and was also a nice height for a man. She was sure, when it happened, that he and Annie would have beautiful children.

"May I sit next to you, Lady Kitty?" Captain Aubrey asked, startling Kitty as she didn't know he was there.

She clutched her bible to her chest as she nodded. "Of course," she smiled kindly. "Do you have a bible?"

He shook his head. "No ... I mean, I do have one, but home in Kent, not here."

"Well you may share mine," she concluded. "Mama gave us each one when we were born. She had our names embroidered into the front with gold thread – do you see?" she asked holding up the bible to see. There below the 'Holy Bible' title read Catherine Kassandra Alcott.

"Kassandra?" he furrowed his brows. "That is an unusual name, what made your parents choose it?"

"Kassandra is a dear friend of my parent's. She and her husband are like family to us. It's a very romantic story, before my brother and I were born, we are twins you know, Kassandra was my mother's ladies maid and Peter was my father's valet. Long story short they fell in love and moved to Nottingham to start their own farm and raise a family. We see them every year at Christmas when we travel to Yorkshire to visit my grandmamma." Kitty loved hearing about what her parents were like before she and her siblings were born. Once they married they were apparently inseparable and they still were.

"I didn't realise that you and your brother were twins," he said, sounding amazed as he led her inside the church.

"I'm glad, it means we do not look similar," Kitty giggled. "I would have been insulted if you had said otherwise." Her family filed into the pew in the front row so that they could sit by Annie, who, as the reverend's wife, sat before her husband.

As the room settled, Joseph took his place at the lectern before the people. "Good morning, everyone, I'm so happy to see you all here looking so well," he said sounding a little nervous. "Today's sermon, or should I say lesson, is inspired by one of my favourite biblical passages. Will everyone open their bibles to Corinthians 13:4?" he asked politely.

The sounds of bibles flipping filled the church as Kitty opened her bible to Corinthians and scanned the pages until she came to the passage that Reverend Preston had asked them to find. As she began to read the passage the realised exactly what the sermon was about. Love.

"Love is patient," Joseph began to read. "Love is kind. It does not envy, it does not boast, it is not proud. It does not dishonour others, it is not self-seeking, it is not easily angered, it keeps no record of wrongs. Love does not delight in evil but rejoices with the truth. It always protects, always trusts, always hopes, always perseveres. Love never fails."

There that word was again – protect.

"Love is a gift," Joseph began to read his sermon. "It is a gift that not everyone is fortunate enough to receive. It is a gift that we must be grateful for and it is a gift that we must give to others. If we are lucky enough to receive this gift we must be careful and gracious and allow room to grow and prosper.

When we are grateful we do not refuse God's gift by dishonouring and betraying love. It is the ultimate sin. We do not covet and steal; instead we cherish and protect the person who has chosen us as their companion and partner.

But as we cherish and protect, we must learn to forgive the wrongdoings of others. Love is flawed, it is not perfect, and it requires effort and time to keep it strong. We must have faith that God knows what's best for us. We must have faith that there is a plan. If we feel pain it is only because God knows you are strong enough to get through it so that we can experience the good there is to come. Love is faith."

For the first time in however many years of churchgoing, Kitty listened to the Reverend's entire sermon. Not only that but she took everything on board. She could actually relate to what he was saying. Everything Joseph said was true. It was valid and it applied to her. She now knew things weren't just handed to her. She wasn't born to privilege for no reason, she wasn't eternally fortunate. There was a plan.

She stole a glance to her side and saw how Captain Aubrey was engrossed in the sermon as well. He was the type of person who would not only protect, but he would cherish and forgive. He was not the type of person who would ever dishonour or betray anyone, let alone the woman he loved. He cared for people, something that she knew not many people did. Without even knowing her he'd saved what could have been a deeply tarnished reputation.

A smile spread across Kitty's face when she realised the source of her admiration for Captain Aubrey – it was romantic affection. He was ever so handsome and terribly genuine. There was still over a month left of the summer season, which meant a month of balls and parties in which a couple could court and get to know each other to see if they were compatible as a potential married couple. But that couldn't happen between them as he would be gone in five days. He would be travelling across the sea into a world of pirates and hurricanes and guns and fighting. There were always tales of ships being destroyed on the ocean but she never worried about it because it was so far away and it didn't affect her. Captain Aubrey's influence had shown her that one had to care about others, even if they didn't know of affect you. Not only was Captain Aubrey sailing into danger himself, but he was sailing with a whole crew of men that had mothers and fathers and sisters and brothers and wives and children, and that worried her. She worried for the families as well as herself.

There was a good chance that when Friday came, it could very be the last time that she ever saw Captain William Aubrey.

Tears flooded her eyes as Reverend Preston began the last part of their church service.

"Will everyone bow their heads in prayer?" he asked.

Simultaneously, everyone in the church bowed their heads and closed their eyes. Kitty took a deep breath as she bowed her head toward the floor.

"Lord," Joseph began. "We ask today not for material things, we ask for guidance. We ask that you guide us in finding the one person who you plan to unite us with. We ask that you give us the courage to forgive once we have found them. We ask that you give us the ability to cherish what we have and no covet what we don't. We ask that you help us to be patient and we ask that you forgive us when we are not. And lastly we acknowledge the presence of our brave naval troops in your house, Lord, and we ask that you guide them safely on their journey and ensure their safe return. In Jesus' name we pray, amen."

"Amen," repeated the entire church. Kitty looked up and knitted her fingers together nervously.

"I hope God's on our side on this voyage," Captain Aubrey whispered, more to himself than to his present company.

"I'll pray for you," Kitty said softly. She wasn't sure if she wanted him to hear her vulnerable statement or not but he did.

"Do not spend your days thinking about me, Lady Kitty," he replied quietly. "I'm sure there will be more exciting things happening to occupy your time. Besides, I don't know if I'll ever be returning to London. We can't predict where the navy will be sent and for how long."

Kitty felt her insides slump as he spoke those words. Just as she'd experienced an element of realisation and self fulfilment, Captain Aubrey had corrected her. Even if he survived, he might not return.

"Go with God's love," Joseph announced and everyone began to rise from their seats on the pews.

As Kitty stood she immediately stumbled with the sudden pain that came with the movement of the areas that were injured during her attack. Captain Aubrey steadied her and her family began asking questions about her wellbeing.

She stared down at Captain Aubrey's hands which were still on her waist, the waist that was not restricted with a corset. He knew that she was not properly dressed.

"I am fine," she said exasperatedly to her family. "Please leave me be."

Before she exited the church to locate the carriage she walked up to her brother – in – law with a self conscious hand still on her waist. Joseph looked surprised to see her which she couldn't blame him for. On a Sunday Kitty got out of church as quickly as she could. He was standing at the door farewelling his congregation.

"Lady Kitty," he smiled at her kindly. "How did you find my sermon?"

"Joseph, we are family, there is no need for titles and aristocratic distinction. I am Kitty, just Kitty," she clarified. "As to your sermon, I can honestly say that I have never not felt lethargic in church before."

Joseph furrowed his brows and pursed his lips. "Am I to say 'thank you'?" he asked.

Kitty laughed lightly. "It was wonderful, I commend you. It was very … applicable," she told him.

Joseph smiled slightly. "Applicable?" he asked. "Will you be in need of my services for matrimonial reasons?"

Kitty shook her head immediately. "It is clear that that is out of the question," she sighed.

"You know, Kitty, being a man of the church, I am trustworthy. Anything you say to me will remain between us, you needn't worry about Annie finding out anything," he assured her.

Kitty leaned up and kissed him on the cheek. "I'll keep it in mind, Joseph," she said truthfully. She would take him up on his offer one day. She could tell that one day she would be in need of a confidante. "We will see you this week for dinner," she said as she walked outside into the lovely mid afternoon sun.

Even after the sermon she could feel the dispersing peoples' eyes on her. Whether they were judgmental or not, she did not know, but it did not stop her from being aware of it.

"You would tell me, or someone, if you were hurting, wouldn't you, Lady Kitty?" said Captain Aubrey as he came up behind her. "I do not want to seem like I am being inappropriate but you are not wearing a corset ..."

Kitty spun around quickly and glared at him warningly. "I do not want to repeat myself again, Captain," she said harshly, refusing to use his Christian name as he had instructed. "I am fine. What does it matter to you, anyway?" she demanded. "It does not bother you that you might not be returning to London, same as it does not bother you that you have someone praying for you." Kitty saw her family exiting the church as they were saying goodbye to Annie and Joseph.

"What right have you to say that I do not care?" he asked in disbelief, recapturing her attention. "How could you presume such a thing? Have I not proven myself to you?"

"Proven yourself?" she repeated. "Why are you trying to prove yourself?"

His blue eyes narrowed. "Perhaps you are more naïve and young than I thought."

Chapter 9

K itty scoffed in disbelief. "Naïve?" she asked as her eyebrows rose. Had she not just informed him that she would be praying for him? How could that have been naïve?

Captain Aubrey sighed and shook his head. "Do not fret about it, Lady Kitty, just forget I said anything. I must take my leave now anyway. I'm due for a meeting with my men." With that he departed the churchyard muttering something to himself.

Kitty was fuming. He hadn't explained himself. How could he call her such things without explaining his meaning? Kitty was immediately intercepted by Evangeline who had been sitting in church with her family. Evangeline immediately wrapped her arms around Kitty tightly. "Oh, darling, I heard what happened to you. Mama was talking to Lady Henrietta whose housemaid is the sister of Lady Russel's ladies maid." Evangeline pulled away and cupped Kitty's face.

Kitty knew it was only a matter of time before the rumours travelled around London. "What did you hear?" she asked Evangeline.

Her hazel eyes softened. "That Sir Walter ..." she looked both sides before whispering "Soiled you."

Kitty's eyes narrowed. "Lies," she hissed to her friend in a hushed tone. "He tried but failed."

Evangeline furrowed her brows. "You fought him? He is twice your width, Kitty!" she exclaimed.

Kitty subconsciously looked after Captain Aubrey but he had already disappeared down the street toward the harbour. "Captain Aubrey came to my rescue," she informed her absently. As displeased as she was in him calling her naiver, she would not deny the fact that he had saved her.

"Your rescue!" Evangeline beamed. "Oh, how positively marvellous. Darling, you must tell me all about it. Do you expect a proposal?" she asked excitedly.

Kitty rolled her eyes. "Really, Eva, must we speak of men as if they are good for only one thing?" she asked, disgruntled.

Evangeline looked slightly hurt at her friend's sudden outburst. "Forgive me, Kitty, I meant no offense. I just wanted to see if you were alright. I also wanted to inform you that the baronet, Charles Ford, who has been residing with us, at my father's insistence, has just asked to court me." Evangeline looked a little embarrassed at her announcement.

Kitty felt horrid. Evangeline had been her closest friend for years. She knew every thought that passed through her head and they trusted each other immensely. "No, you must forgive me, Eva. I'm sorry for my ugly behaviour. Now, about this baronet – is he handsome?" she asked, trying to change the subject.

Evangeline pointed over to where her family was standing, conversing with a handsome young man whom Kitty presumed to be the baronet. His hair was a light red colour and his clothes spoke of money. He appeared to be quite well mannered as his posture was perfect and he was impeccably groomed.

"He told me that I was a vision," she whispered.

Kitty could agree that Evangeline certainly was very beautiful. "Then he is a wise man," she smiled at her friend. "I congratulate you, Eva, and I look forward to attending your nuptials. I trust they will be before the season is up? There is nothing I love more than a summer wedding. You will be the envy of every young debutante."

"I hope you are right," Evangeline sighed.

Kitty noticed her family entering their carriages. "I must go, I will see you soon," she told her friend.

"Will you be attending the naval ball on Thursday? My father tells me it is a 'farewell' of sorts," Evangeline asked.

Kitty pursed her lips as she went to walk away. "I'm not sure, my father wants to restrict our time at the summer festivities. After last night he is quite reserved about me being out in society. I was only worried about the rumours … it seems that several ladies are already speaking about me already."

Evangeline shook her head. "You know me, darling, and therefore you know how fast I can spread word. I will have this righted in no time, I promise you."

"Thank you, Eva," Kitty said sincerely. She didn't want incorrect whispers spreading around London that painted her as promiscuous. She then walked swiftly over to her family who were waiting for her beside their carriages.

"Where is the Captain?" her mother asked her, looking around.

Kitty shrugged her shoulders. "He's gone to prepare for his voyage, it seems to be the only thing he cares about," she mumbled under her breath. She climbed into the smaller carriage so that she was with her sister and Sabine and not her parents who would no doubt ask questions.

As the carriage took off, Sabine and Little J stared at her curiously. Kitty sighed and looked up at them. "What?" she snapped.

"We're not going to ask you what you and Captain Aubrey were discussing. We don't know that whatever it was has put you in a foul mood just as we don't know what you're completely besotted with him," Little J said carefully.

Kitty rolled her eyes. "Really covert, Little J," she scoffed.

"She's just trying to help," Sabine said sadly. "We both are. We know that you fancy the Captain and he too fancies you. But he's travelling on Friday ... do you really think that it is wise to promise yourself to him when he will be gone for so long?"

"There has been no promise of anything," Kitty clarified. "Nor has there been any talk of affections. He called me ... naïve."

"Of the three of us, you are the least naïve," Little J assured her. "In what context was it said?"

Kitty sighed. "He said 'have I not proven myself?' to me. What does that even mean?"

Sabine smiled slightly. "Perhaps you are naïve," she said comically. "He's trying to impress you. I suppose you are used to fancy balls and formal courtships."

"Impress me?" Kitty repeated, taken aback. "He saved me from Sir Walter, which was being gentlemanly and kind."

"Kitty, here's where being cleverer than everyone else comes in handy," Little J said leaning forward. "Captain Aubrey adores you. You reciprocate those feelings, my dear, and you both need to stop being foolish. I want you to be happy, but you can't know whether this connection will be smart as he is going away for so long."

Were they right? Was everything he'd done all to impress her? Did he really have such affection for her? She knew how she felt about him; he was the only man that she had ever felt had not seen her as one who they could conquer.

"I think I'm falling in love with him," Kitty whispered. No matter what he did or said, he would always be that man who made her feel like she was more than a pretty face.

She saw both Sabine and Little J's jaws drop in shock. The identical expressions on each of their faces were quite amusing to Kitty considering she'd just revealed something intensely personal.

"Love?" they both exclaimed.

Kitty nodded helplessly. "I don't know how to describe it. He makes me feel safe and secure and that if I strive to be more than a silly flirt than I can be great. At the same time he frustrates me and he makes no sense when he talks to me. He uses Greek mythology analogies to make sense of regular situations and he looks and the stars and makes them seem magical and his mother was like me and ..." she ranted before her sister cut her off.

"Kitty," Little J said quickly to get her to quieten down.

Kitty gasped slightly as she regained her breath.

"Kitty, you don't need to prove anything to us. If you think that a courtship could start and remain strong though his voyage then who are we to stop you?" Sabine said sincerely. "We're supporting you no matter what."

Kitty's stomach felt heavy as the realisation filled her. She felt incredibly vulnerable. Vulnerability was not something that she was familiar with nor was the comfortable with feeling it.

It was foreign to her as she had never had genuine romantic feelings for a man. Or rather she'd never allowed herself to have genuine romantic feelings for a man. She'd always been too preoccupied with having fun with Evangeline to actually think about marriage.

"Lord, marriage," she gasped, without realising she'd said it out loud.

"What?" Little J furrowed her eyebrows.

"Did you say 'marriage'?" Sabine added.

Kitty's eyes widened. "No," she said quickly. She silently thanked God when she felt the carriage come to a halt outside Ethridge Manor. "Oh, look," she chirped. "We're home!"

"This conversation isn't over, Catherine!" Little J called after Kitty as she quickly scampered from the carriage.

She quickly made her way up the stairs and shut herself in her room, locking the door behind her. She had two things to do that day. The first was to change out of her Sunday clothes and into a nice gown that made her look conservative yet lovely … and go down to the Royal Rose and visit Captain Aubrey. She needed to apologise for doubting him, but she also needed to ask him a very important question.

Chapter 10

William couldn't believe how stupid he'd been to even entertain the thought of a romance with Lady Kitty. It wasn't right for many reasons. First and foremost, he did not have a title or a home to offer her. Second, she was a beautiful, young debutante who most likely had more desirable suitors and third, she was more naïve and innocent than he had originally thought.

Walking away from the church he felt like a great fool. He'd been trying to prove himself worthy of her all week. He'd been trying to change her to show her how lovely she was when she was just being herself, and not the silly girl she was at parties.

He could see the change she had made in the short amount of time she had been trying, she was really making an effort and he appreciated that. And that's where it all had gone sour. It was hard for William not to shake with anger as he pictured Sir Walter with his hands on Kitty. It had taken every ounce of strength within him not to quickly flick his wrist and watch Sir Walter bleed to death, but if he'd done that he would hang and not him. Even so, the man still walked free.

The way she had looked at him afterward though made him sure that even she, the beautiful Lady Kitty Alcott fancied him. Kitty trusted him, and that was something he knew she would not be able to do with many men after what she had been through.

"I should not have been so short with her," he said to himself as he walked towards the docks. "It is not a crime to be oblivious to a man's intentions, especially when he is a blind fool like me." He knew he had not been clear with his intentions. He was not good at expressing his feelings, especially towards someone like Kitty Alcott, who was beautiful in every sense of the word.

The first time he had seen her in that ballroom he had felt something inside of him change. She was stunning, the loveliest girl he had ever laid his eyes on. Her hair was chocolate brown and so clean and shiny and her eyes were the strangest shade of dark blue that he'd ever seen so it made her completely unique. But then he had seen how she behaved in public. He did not dismiss her for his own enjoyment; he wanted it to be a wakeup call to her. She didn't need to flirt and tease to receive attention; he knew she was better than that. And it had seemed to work.

William felt as though he had changed as well. He was no longer so self - orientated. He'd never worried about another human being before ... not like the way he worried about Kitty. He worried about his parents if ever the rains were particularly ferocious and his father was out on the sea and he worried about his crew whenever they ventured into dangerous waters, but he'd never worried about someone like Kitty.

The thought of something bad happening to her was unbearable. If he'd arrived a few minutes later to find Sir Walter raping her then he would have felt as though he'd failed her in every way a man could fail a woman. He had to protect her, there was no other way. She was it; she was the only one he would ever worry about from this day on. If she was gone ... then he might as well be gone too.

But how could he ever ponder these feelings when he was about to ship out for a very long time. It was a miracle if they ever made port in England, let alone London. He was being ridiculous.

His men, as previously organised, had gathered at the Royal Rose. They had either been staying aboard the ship, with hosts or at various brothels that doubled as hotels. Several months at sea made a man yearn for female company. William, himself, had never been to brothel not did he ever plan to. He felt sorry for the women there. His parents had raised him to treat women with respect, and that was something he strived to do.

As he arrived at the Royal Rose he felt a sense of doom. Not because she was a bad vessel, on the contrary, she was one of His Majesty's finest, but because he knew she would be taking him away from where he wanted to be. Not even the familiar smell of the salty sea air could calm him.

He walked up the ramp to the deck of the ship and his crew stopped what they were doing immediately and stood up straight to receive their Captain. They all saluted him and he returned the gesture. William cared about respect. He felt if he showed his men respect then they would show the same respect for him.

"I trust you've all had a very productive time in London while we've had our toes on land," he began. He noticed several of the men share a few obvious looks but he ignored them. "But it's time again for us to make sail once again. We are not heading off to battle against the armada or anything exciting like that, we are simply escorting British trade ships as they journey to both America and the Caribbean."

His second in command, Commander George Gates, stepped forward. "Sir," he said formally. "Why is a hundred and twenty gunner escorting a trade ship?"

"Commander, I'm following orders. The King wants these routes safe. Three trade ships in the past year have been intercepted by pirates and all sorts of criminals so it will be our responsibility to ensure their safe arrival," William explained patiently. Commander Gates was a very noble and loyal naval officer. It would not be long before he was in control of his own ship in the royal navy.

"Of course, sir," the Commander conceded stepping back to where he was before.

"We ship out Friday. So break the hearts of those women you've soiled and be ready to depart at dawn that day." William turned to the three Lieutenants he had aboard the ship - Peter, John and Benjamin. "I want the cannons cleaned and stocked. I want whatever weight that is not necessary to be left here as I want this journey to be as swift and as quick as possible."

The three Lieutenants nodded obediently before leaving to go below deck.

"Return to your duties," William instructed to the rest of his men. "I don't want to see one loose rope when we depart. The Royal Rose is the beauty of the King's ships and I want her to live up to her reputation." It was true. The ship was named for the King's niece and she was a beauty, or so he was told.

The crew dispersed all except for Commander Gates. The man was a little older than William's nine and twenty years. He wasn't sure how old, but the Commander's green eyes were definitely wise.

"Captain, are you expecting anyone?" he asked knowingly.

William furrowed his eyebrows. "What are you insinuating, Commander?"

"Nothing, sir, I'm merely asking as an incredibly pampered princess is standing on the dock looking lost. She looks like the type of woman that you would take a fancy to ... she reminds me of that young lady I was once involved with in France. She didn't speak one word of English but she loved every part of me," the Commander smiled as he peered over the side of the ship. "If you don't mind I might say my English farewells in her company. The wind is being kind to our eyes, you can see her ankles."

William curiously looked down to the dock to see Kitty looking round with a confused expression on her face. She had changed from her Sunday best into a lovely pink gown that accentuated her narrow waist. She wore a matching bonnet with her hair in neat ringlets down her back. Expensive white lace was sewn into the neckline of her gown which made her look conservatively pretty. Commander Gates was correct about the wind. The sea breeze was blowing her skirts up around her ankles. She was twirling her parasol repetitively which William thought was a sign of her anxiety.

"You even think about touching her and you will be demoted to naval cadet so fast that your head will spin ... and that's just what I will do to you professionally," William threatened furiously. He hadn't realised that he'd been gripping the side of the boat so hard that the wood had begun to splinter.

Commander Gates backed away from him. "I'm sorry, sir, I didn't realise that she was yours."

"One cannot own a woman, Commander, we can only hope to be worthy of her choosing us. When a woman like her gives you her heart, it is once in a lifetime," he said distantly as he watched Kitty. She still had not noticed him and was still looking around the docks. Clearly she was not aware of which vessel was the Royal Rose. There were several ships moored to the dock, but none as grand as his vessel.

"You speak fine poetry, Captain," he commended him. "Have you asked her to wait for you?"

"It happens once in a lifetime, Commander," William told Commander Gates. "But not in my lifetime. Excuse me." He left the Commander and walked over to the ramp to go back down to the dock. Kitty had already walked down the dock to a passenger ship that was bound for America in the next few days. "Kitty!" he called out.

She immediately spun around and smiled brilliantly at him. To see that look on her face nearly killed him. He knew that it was highly likely that once they departed that Friday he might never see it again. "You're here!" she exclaimed. She held the bonnet to her head and she walked as quickly as possible over to him.

He paused. They'd parted when he had behaved quite temperamentally with her.

When she joined him her chest was rising and falling quite quickly which told him she was quite excited ... either that or she was nervous.

"Lady Kitty," he began. "What are you doing here?"

"I managed to slip out of the house unnoticed so papa could not insist on a chaperone ... I know what you will think - 'Kitty, you're being irresponsible. Aren't you concerned about what happened with Sir Walter?' - but I don't need one with you. I feel safe with you," she said with a wide smile on her face. She closed her parasol and tightened her hands around it.

"I didn't mean about the lack of a chaperone," William rephrased. "I meant what are you doing here? Why have you come to my ship?"

Kitty pursed her lips while her dark blue eyes sparkled. "You are the only man who has ever treated me with the respect I now know I deserve. It is not very ladylike of me and I know that and I know you're leaving on Friday but I want you to know," she said nervously, her voice cracking slightly. "If you want, and you're absolutely not under any obligation to accept, but if you want, you have someone to write to, you have someone who is thinking of you and you have someone who is waiting for you."

He could have danced he was so happy, he could have sung, as what she was saying was fulfilling his wildest dreams. But he couldn't ask her to wait for him when there was a chance he might not come back. It wasn't fair for someone so young to take a chance on something that was not a sure thing.

"Kitty, I'm not going on a holiday and coming back in a few months," he said regretfully. "I might not come back."

Kitty's eyes immediately glistened with fresh tears. "If you think like that then you expect it," she whispered.

William looked around to make sure that there wasn't an audience. He took her gloved hand and pulled her quickly underneath the ramp up to the Royal Rose. A dark shadow cast over her face once they had disappeared from the public's eye. "I'm being realistic, Lady Kitty, I won't pretend otherwise."

"You don't want me?" she asked in a heartbreaking tone.

The question nearly killed William to hear. More than anything he would have liked to answer - 'I do want you. Most ardently, my darling' - but he couldn't. It wasn't fair. "Kitty, you've said before that I've protected you. That is what I'm doing now."

Kitty's eyes narrowed. "You didn't answer my question," she pointed out. "Must you be such a gentleman all the time?" she asked exasperatedly.

William couldn't control himself. It was as if his hands and his body had taken over his mind and his good sense. He grabbed her quickly, yet softly as not to hurt her tender sides. He could feel again that she was not wearing a corset which showed him that she was an injury as a result of her attack.

Placing one hand on her waist and the other on her cheek he pressed his lips to hers. She responded immediately, wrapping her arms around his neck, holding him tightly.

The way she smelt, the way she felt, the sounds she made ... it all made him want to lose control. But he couldn't, he would not be like Sir Walter and push her into anything. He released her and stepped back.

Once again her chest was rising and falling as she breathed quickly. Her cheeks were red with blush and her lips were plump with his kiss.

"I am no gentleman," William said, realising he too was out of breath.

Kitty grinned devilishly. "You were right, Captain Aubrey, the next person I kissed would be the one I was in love with," she said smiling.

Chapter 11

Inside, Kitty was dying. He was just staring at her. They were standing under a damp wooden ramp on the edge of London and he'd just kissed her. She'd professed her love for him and he was just staring.

His bright blue eyes were wide. Kitty couldn't determine whether they were wide with embarrassment or sheer pity. She stepped away from him until her head was touching the ramp. She fidgeted with her gown anxiously and then began to straighten the lace on her parasol. 'Be calm,' she told herself. 'He'll leave in a moment and you'll be clear to run away.'

It was at least five minutes before he said anything. "Why?" was all he managed to say.

Kitty was surprised. Off all things to say, she wasn't expecting a simple question. At least he wasn't demanding her to leave him alone. "Why what?" she said softly.

Captain Aubrey smiled slightly and shook his head. He ran a hand through his thick, dark blond hair and then laughed lightly. "Why is this happening to me now?" he asked as if it were the simplest question in the world.

Kitty didn't know whether she was supposed to be offended. "You were the one who kissed me. You told me that my first kiss would be with the one I love, and it was. I didn't realise that he would find me so … laughable."

Captain Aubrey closed the distance between them and placed his hands lightly on her waist. Kitty was well aware of the fact that he knew she was not properly dressed in her underclothes, she, however, appreciated the fact that he knew it was because of an injury. "Why is this happening to me now?" he repeated with a smile on his face. "I'm leaving in five days. Why could this have not happened when my duty was over so I could do something about it?"

Kitty peered up at him curiously. "You're not angry?"

He shook his head. "I'm much happier than I ought to be. You deserve far better than me, Kitty."

Kitty was confused. "How can you say that?" she asked. "What is wrong with you?"

"Many things," he chuckled. "The first is that I'm besotted with a woman far above my station."

Kitty could feel her heart swell. He reciprocated. He felt the same way. She wasn't insane. She now knew how her mother felt about her father, how her Aunt Jane felt about her Uncle Daniel, how her grandmamma had felt about her grandpapa … a feeling that was completely indescribable. If he were not holding her to the ground she was sure she might fly.

"Stations do not matter when it comes to love," she informed him excitedly. "Why, my father was just a small town solicitor when he inherited the earldom and married my mama … that's not a good example … er … my aunt! My

Aunt Jane was just a farmer's daughter when she married my uncle, the Earl of Southerby."

Captain Aubrey smiled sadly at her. "That's different, Kitty. He was the one with the money and the grand estate to offer her. With us it is the other way around."

"Money does not matter," Kitty assured him.

"Says the girl who has never lived without it, the girl who has never wanted for anything," he pressed. "I have money, Kitty, but not nearly enough to give you your lifestyle."

Kitty sighed, frustrated. Why must all marriage negotiations be about money? "I don't need my lifestyle," she sighed.

Captain Aubrey shook his head solemnly. "You may think that now, but after months of living in a modest house with only a scullery maid and a cook for a household you will resent me for it."

"I have a dowry," she informed him. "A handsome one," she continued. "The reverend received eight thousand pounds when he married Annie. Would that not suffice?"

"I will not take your father's money," he said firmly.

"That's what Joseph said," she recalled. "Papa insisted though, so Joseph set aside a few thousand pounds for the education and futures of their children and donated the rest to the poor."

He released her waist and rubbed his hands together that made Kitty think that he was anxious. "You remind me of my naval cadets. They arrive so amazed at the crisp new uniform and the fancy, gold hilted sword on their hip – everything is new and exciting. And then they experience their first battle. They see cannon balls destroying beautiful ships and destroying young lives. Their innocence is gone and they realise how serious life is."

"I suppose a cadet is better than a vain Greek queen," Kitty mumbled, wondering where he was going with his story.

Captain Aubrey caressed her cheek lightly. "I would rather leave you on Friday knowing that you never hated me then promise you something that you would resent me for later."

Kitty huffed impatiently. "Are you finished?" she said icily.

He nodded looking a little taken aback at her sudden mood change.

"Do not make my decisions for me, Captain, and do not pretend to know what I will and will not do. How could you possibly predict that I would resent you? My grandmamma lives by herself on her farm in Yorkshire. We spend every winter there. She doesn't have maids or cooks so I know exactly what I would expect. I've cooked ... granted, not well, but I can improve, and I've cleaned. I've cared for animals and I've sewn clothes. There is a whole other side of me that you do not know, Captain." Kitty placed her hands on her hips and awaited his response. She was quite proud of herself. "My little sister went from being Lady Anne to being Mrs Annie Preston and she's doing perfectly."

Captain Aubrey appeared to concede. "Perhaps I was mistaken. I do not pretend to know what you will and won't do. I think it's clear that there is no way of knowing what will happen next with you, Lady Kitty, but I know I'm curious. There is one crucial difference between the good reverend and me. There is no possibility of him being hollowed out by a cannon ball."

The hideous image filled Kitty's mind. She could see the violent setting so vividly. She could see his bright blue eyes becoming dull as he died. Kitty felt as though she would be sick. "How can you be blasé?" she whispered.

"Forgive me, I'm sorry," he apologised quickly, wrapping his arms around her securely. Kitty enjoyed the feeling of being in his arms. It allowed her to calm herself after the horrendous thought. "It is what I mentally prepare myself for. I know I will see blood, so I expect the worst and hope for the best."

Kitty closed her eyes as she leant against his chest. "I would not care if I lived on ten thousand pounds a year or ten pounds a year. This feeling, this all consuming feeling, I have is worth more than every penny I've ever had."

She felt his lips brush the top of her hair. "I leave in five days. I will be gone for months and even then I am not sure when I will return to England."

"Why don't you retire?" Kitty suggested already knowing the answer.

"My sweet, the navy is all I've ever known. What will I do if I retire?" he asked her.

"Do not call me that," Kitty said quickly. "It is what my papa calls my mama whenever he is trying to be romantic." She shuddered. "But, you could do what my papa used to do. Become a solicitor."

"Something that does not involve me sitting in an office," he laughed. "My mother had a hard enough time teaching me how to read and write when I was a boy. All I did was want to be out on the water with my father," he recalled happily.

"Why don't you do that then? Become a fisherman," she prompted. "Or, if you do not want to leave the navy completely, become one of the men that trains the cadets in England – there are those sorts of men, aren't there?"

"I'll find something to do," he assured her. He touched her cheek again softly. "If I was a better man I would tell you to find someone else. You are far too young to be tying yourself to someone like me."

Kitty rolled her eyes. "Someone like you? What is wrong with you, pray tell?"

"It would be easier for you to marry a man like your father … a man who will inherit a grand estate and has a house full of servants," he sighed.

"That would be easier," Kitty nodded. "And a man like my father is perfect … but I wouldn't be happy with that, as I won't be happy with anyone but you. You are perfect for me. I know you're leaving in five days, but distance does not matter."

Captain Aubrey smiled down at her. "I will return to you," he promised. "But right now you must return home before your father discovers you've left the house without a chaperone. I would escort you but I can't leave my men. I want you to walk straight home, the most direct way, you understand?" he instructed and Kitty nodded. "Do not stop to talk to anyone."

Kitty bit her lip nervously. "I don't want to be presumptuous," she stammered. "But … are we engaged?"

"I will not propose to you underneath a ramp on a dock. I will propose to you the way you deserve," he promised her. He leant down and kissed her on the forehead. "I will be at

Ethridge later. Do not speak of this to anyone before I have an opportunity to ask your father's permission."

Kitty beamed up at him. Was it truly possible that everything could go right for her and William? Could she possibly have everything? "I'll see you later, Captain," she smiled coyly at him. As she went to turn away to go back out from under the ramp she felt him catch her arm. She looked back at him to see his blue eyes looking quite glassy.

"If I'm to be your husband, you mustn't call me 'Captain,'" he winked at her.

Kitty couldn't help the embarrassing red blush that filled her cheeks as she dashed away from him. She immediately put up her parasol and looked around to see if anyone had seen her emerge from the ramp after her interlude with Captain Aubrey. The men, both naval and otherwise, were going about their business, not bothering to look up at her. Gathering up her skirts she walked as swiftly as she could away from the docks. Such a place was not one where a lady was usually seen.

Even while trying to remain conspicuous she could not wipe the smile off her face. Her risk of revealing her feelings to Captain Aubrey had paid off. He loved her too. She realised that he was right, when they were married she couldn't keep referring to him as 'Captain' ... she had to think of him as 'William.

It seemed ridiculous that it was only a short time ago that she loathed the man that her father had brought into their home. And now she couldn't imagine how she was going to survive months on end without word from him. She was sure he would write whenever they made port but even then, that could be ages before she heard anything from him.

She did just as William had instructed her. She went straight home and was vigilant in not making eye contact with anyone. Once she reached Ethridge Manor she was going to slip inside the servant's entrance and sneak through the kitchens and then go above stairs as if she'd never left in the first place.

Once she arrived home she was sure that nothing could spoil her mood. She opened the large, gothic style gate and then stopped in her tracks. Nothing could spoil her mood ... except that.

Her father looked ropable. His dark blue eyes that so mirrored her own were filled with pure rage. He stood outside the front door with his hands balled into fists at his side.

Kitty nervously closed the gate behind her and walked up to him slowly. "I can explain ..." she began before her father cut her off.

"You bloody better be able to," he growled and he walked down the few stairs to where she was standing. In a matter of seconds he had her flipped off her feet and flung over his shoulder.

"Oof!" Kitty yelped with surprise. The pressure on her waist was excruciating to her but she wasn't about to complain when she was in such trouble with her father. "Papa, put me down!" was all she demanded.

"If you're going to act and defy me like a child, Catherine, then you will be treated like one," he snapped as he carried her inside. The servants stopped their work as they watched the master carry his eldest daughter as if she were a sack of flour.

They came to the stairs and Sebastian made a point to stomp up them and make a scene to let everyone know how displeased he was ... or that was what Kitty's theory was. She stopped fighting and just slumped over his shoulder.

"Sebastian, what are you doing?" her mother exclaimed as they entered the family hallway. Her brothers, Sabine and Little J all came out of their bedchambers to see what she spectacle was.

"Kitty snuck out without a chaperone when she knew full well what the rules were," Sebastian informed his wife distastefully. He opened Kitty's bedchamber door while he balanced his daughter on his shoulder. "I am so disappointed in you, Kitty," he said as he threw her, albeit gently, down onto her bed.

Kitty could see it in his eyes. There was a mixture of fury and disappointment but also fear.

"Papa," Little J said from the door. "It's my fault, I was supposed to go with Kitty and I forgot, I told her to go on ahead but I got immersed in a book," she fibbed as she tried to cover for her sister.

Kitty couldn't believe how loyal her sister was. She wished she could have smiled at her but she wasn't about to get Little J into trouble.

"Go back to your room, Little J, I don't want to be angry with you for lying to me," he snapped at his middle child. He walked over to the door and closed it, making sure she prying eyes of her family were not looking in.

The only decent excuse that Kitty would have was that she was engaged but William had asked her specifically not to tell anyone until he asked her father.

"Papa, I'm sorry," Kitty whispered. "I didn't mean to anger you."

Sebastian spun around and stared at her. "Anger me?" he asked in disbelief. "You're going to put me into an early grave, young lady! This weekend you have scared me more times than I'd ever care to be scared. I don't make rules for my own pleasure, Kitty; they're there for your protection. They're not just you either; they're for your sisters as well."

Kitty felt ashamed that her actions had affected others so. "Papa, I was safe," she whispered.

"You are not safe unless I can see you," he retorted quickly. "Sir Walter is a disgusting man, but there are plenty more like him in the world. Some men just see a pretty girl and they lose control, that's why chaperones have been invented!"

"Papa," Kitty sighed. "I was not wandering around the boroughs at night on my lonesome; I just went for a walk." She would not ever allow herself to be in the same position she was with Sir Walter. She would rather die than feel so powerless again.

"Where?" he demanded to know.

Kitty had to think fast. "The park," she replied.

"Why?"

"I already told you, I went for a walk," Kitty said, frustrated.

"I know that isn't true, Kitty, stop lying to me," Sebastian snapped angrily.

Kitty pouted. "Papa," she choked, feeling the tears coming. "Something wonderful has happened and you're ruining it!" she exclaimed.

"What's happened then, Kitty? If you don't want to spend the rest of your season locked in this room, you will tell me the truth," he instructed seriously.

Kitty couldn't tell him, William had specifically asked her not to. What was an hour in hot water with her father? Once William arrived he would set things right.

"Papa, you will find out in time," she said firmly.

Sebastian rolled his eyes and opened the door. "One day when you're a parent, Kitty, you will understand the necessity of rules. Sometimes I wish I believed in spanking, perhaps it would drill the message into you." With that he was gone and Kitty was alone.

She crawled into the centre of her bed and crossed her legs. "William better plan a very romantic proposal," she said to herself. "Angry Lord Ethridge is not one that I like to deal with."

Chapter 12

William felt physically ill as he arrived back at Ethridge Manor that evening. Organising the men for their voyage had taken longer than he had originally anticipated. He's had to receive coordinates and orders as well as organise supplies to get them to the Caribbean before they could resupply.

It was well after nightfall and he was sure that the Alcott's had already eaten their supper. He wanted to talk to Sebastian though he was sure that he had retired for the night. He walked in the door at Ethridge at around midnight and Mr Carter offered to have some food taken to his bedchamber which he thanked him for.

Just having one man wait on him made him realise how used to such comforts he was already, and he had only been residing there for a short time. Kitty had grown up with it her entire life. Could she really just abandon everything she knew?

He decided to go down to the kitchens to eat his food so maids and footmen didn't have to be woken in order for them to bring it to him. In doing so it meant he walked past Sebastian's private study.

The door was ajar and he could hear the sound of glass clinking. William peered inside curiously and sure enough, Sebastian was sitting on his settee holding a bottle of whiskey in one hand and a glass in the other. He was wearing a dark robe of his nightclothes and his hair was untidy, as if he had been to bed and couldn't sleep.

"Lord Ethridge?" William said cautiously.

Sebastian turned his head to see William standing in the doorway. He smiled and beckoned him inside. "We missed you at dinner," he commented. "Em has grown quite fond of you … I'm wondering if I should be jealous."

William laughed lightly at the idea. "You are the only man for Lady Ethridge, my Lord," he assured him.

Sebastian smiled to himself and nodded. "I don't know what I did right in my life to get her, but clearly someone up there was looking out for me when they sent me her," he told him, gesturing to the heavens.

"I would love to be as fortunate as you have been one day, my Lord," William said honestly.

"You will be," Sebastian promised. "There is one woman out there for everyone; I'd like to believe that. Emilia is my match in every way. I have had a blessed life. I have a beautiful wife and five healthy children. I should be happy," he said sadly.

William furrowed his eyebrows and walked further into the room, closing the doors behind him. Was it the drink talking? "Are you alright, Lord Ethridge?" he asked, concerned.

Sebastian held the bottle of whiskey up to William. "Would you like a drink?" he offered.

William shook his head. "I'm not much of a drinker," he replied. He'd seen one too many people act irrationally under the influence of alcohol.

"Neither am I," he sighed and placed the glass and the bottle on the floor beside the settee. "I haven't had a drop; I just thought it might make things a little easier. Truth be told, the whiskey belonged to the last Earl. Would you take a seat?" he offered William the settee sitting opposite him.

William sat down cautiously and watched the Earl as he closed his eyes. The man did look like someone had punched him in the gut. "What is wrong, sir, if I may ask?"

"I love my family with everything I have. I would kill for them and I would die for them. It just hurts me to know that they ... I think they resent me. James is put out as I have barred his usual escapades this summer. Little J ... I don't know what she does all day but all I know is that she doesn't trust me or her mother enough to confide in. Henry, well Henry is a good boy; I don't have to worry about him. He does his schoolwork and he treats women with respect and that's all I ask. Annie I know is struggling as she hasn't fallen pregnant ... and perhaps it is because I am a man that she does not talk to me but I was with Emilia through all the hard times when it came to birthing.

And then there is Kitty. I don't know what to do with her. She deliberately disobeyed me, you said it yourself, she needs to grow up and I don't know how to make her without changing her and I don't want her to be anyone but herself. I was furious today when I found out she snuck out of the house without a chaperone when I specifically said that nobody was to be without a chaperone when they left the house. Kitty is who I worry about most. I feel as though she hates me for ruining her season and her freedom and her social life. I love her … I love them all so much but they kill me." Sebastian slumped down on the settee and rubbed his temples as if he had a migraine.

William didn't know what to say. Sebastian looked like a broken man. He looked like he truly felt his children hated him.

"Your children love you, Lord Ethridge. They know that everything you do is to protect them," William said weakly, trying to make him feel better.

Sebastian opened his eyes and looked over at William. "You should have seen them when they were small. I used to be able to wrap my arms around them all and lift them up … of course not for a very long time but it still made them all laugh. Sometimes I wish they never grew up and I could continue to be the most important man in their lives."

"You are the most important man in their lives," he said with more assurance in his voice. "They know that whatever happens that they can always come to you. They might not always but they know you're there. It's a comfort to know that, believe me."

"You should have seen the way that Kitty looked at me when I was scolding her. It was a mixture of sadness and humiliation. I really felt as though I lost my little girl."

"You didn't lose me, papa," said a voice in the doorway. Both men turned to see Kitty standing there in her nightdress. Her dark blue eyes were glistening with tears.

William wondered how long she had been standing there and how much she'd heard. He felt terribly guilty for Sebastian's misery over his thoughts on Kitty. It was his fault that she had come out to the docks to see him. If he had not been so short with her then she would not have ventured out alone and disobeyed Sebastian's ruled. In saying that though he was very glad she came to see him, if she had not then he never would have known that she reciprocated his feelings.

Kitty crossed the room in a flash to her father's side, the rags in her hair bouncing as she ran to her father. She wrapped her arms around his neck and hugged him tightly. Sebastian righted himself and pulled his daughter onto his lap as if she were a young girl once more. William found himself smiling at the sight. "You won't ever lose me, papa," Kitty promised.

Sebastian kissed his daughters cheeks as he held her. "You scare me, my darling. Your safety, your life, is more important than any errand you have to run outside the house. Kitty, I always tell you the truth. I've never told you a lie, I only ask that you, and your brothers and sisters extend to me that same courtesy."

Kitty shot a nervous look at William quickly before returning to her father. "It wasn't an errand ..." she started before William cut in.

"It was my fault, Lord Ethridge," William admitted. "That's what I had come in here to tell you. I was quite quick tempered with Kitty after church today so she came down to the docks to rectify our friendship. What we discovered is that our friendship is slightly stronger than we both realised."

Sebastian's eyes widened as he looked from Kitty to William. Kitty beamed and nodded. William noticed that his hands immediately tightened on Kitty. William knew that he would have a hard time letting his daughter go.

"You invited me here with the insinuation that a union between Lady Kitty and myself would be formed. At first I thought that idea was ludicrous, but I couldn't imagine my life without her," he said more to Kitty than to her father. Kitty's face completely softened and she looked at him with love in her eyes. "I know I'm leaving in five days ... well, I believe it's Monday so it is now four days, but I'd like your permission to marry her once I return."

Sebastian pursed his lips and looked William up and down. His eyes were intense and William feared that he would say 'no'. He looked at Kitty and raised his eyebrows. "You're happy?" he asked.

She nodded nervously.

Sebastian's eyes flashed back to William. "I grew up on a Yorkshire farm, Captain Aubrey, so a lot of our food I caught. I skinned many rabbits in my day; the same technique applies when skinning a human. I just won't do you the courtesy of killing you first."

William knew it was a warning. "I won't hurt her, milord," he promised.

"Well then who am I to object?" he smiled and shifted Kitty off his lap. He stood up and held his hand out to William.

William shook his hand excitedly. "Thank you, Lord Ethridge," he said gratefully.

"Sebastian," he corrected. "We are to be family, are we not?"

Kitty squealed with delight. "Thank you, papa!" she pulled him into a tight hug. "Thank you!"

"The chaperone rule still stands, Catherine," Sebastian said sternly.

Kitty nodded profusely. "Of course," she promised.

Sebastian sighed. "Your journey will be a long one," he commented. "That is a long time to wait for a wedding. We could have Joseph marry you on Thursday before you leave and once you return you can have the wedding you always dreamed of."

Kitty's eyes sparkled with delight as she looked at William. "Do you want to?" she asked hopefully.

William could be married by Thursday. The woman of his dreams was standing before him in a nightgown and hair rags and she looked more beautiful than if she were wearing one of her flawless gowns. She was it. She was the one he wanted. And she was willing to marry him even though he would be gone for a very long time. "I cannot wait to call you my wife," he smiled down at her. "Do you think that things could be organised so soon?" he asked Sebastian.

"All Kitty needs is a white dress and we shall be grand. I'm sure you'd like to be married in your uniform?"

Sebastian nodded. "I shall send for my parents immediately," he said eagerly.

Kitty's face dropped. "What about grandmamma?" she exclaimed.

"Grandmamma will be at the grand affair. We do not have time to send a carriage. She would rather help mama plan your wedding then rush into town and possibly miss it," Sebastian assured her. "Speaking of mama, perhaps you should go and wake her and tell her your good news?" he suggested to Kitty.

Kitty but her lip and looked at William as she was about to leave the room. He could tell what she wanted but there was absolutely no way that he was showing any sort of physical affection toward Kitty while her father was in the room.

Sebastian could also tell what his daughter wanted. He let out an exasperated groan and covered his eyes. "You have five seconds," he muttered.

Kitty giggled and quickly wrapped her arms around William's neck. He leant down and quickly kissed her lips, very wary that her father was standing not five feet from them.

"I should like to see you in a white dress," he whispered in her ear.

"Your wish is my command," she said almost seductively. She unwrapped her arms from his neck and quickly scampered out of the room, no doubt to inform Emilia of the developments.

"You should speak to Joseph," Sebastian advised him. "Not for religious enlightenment, but for what it is like to marry into this family. The poor man endured my mother, sister and Emilia all at once. Just think about that when you return, this family does not do a celebration halfway."

"I'll keep that in mind," William grinned. He couldn't believe he was engaged. He needed to write to his parents right away. He had no doubt in his mind that his parents, John and Kathleen Aubrey, would love Kitty.

Chapter 13

F or Kitty, that week passed all too fast. Before she knew it, it was Wednesday and it was time for the ton to get together once again to farewell the naval troops who were going to be gone for quite some time.

True to his word, Sebastian had kept the Alcott family home from the several parties and dinners that they had been invited to and Kitty silently thanked him for it. The time spent at home was the time she spent with her fiancée and that time had been uncomfortable thanks to a conversation Kitty had had with Evangeline.

News of Lady Kitty Alcott's quick engagement to the Captain had caused quite a stir. Rumours were flying about town suggesting that the Captain was being a gentleman after Sir Walter had 'soiled' Lady Kitty, others said that Sebastian had paid the Captain handsomely to wed his ruined daughter just in case she was with child.

Immediately after it was announced, Evangeline had called on Kitty to hear all the gossip. William had been blind sighted by the sudden appearance of the energetic Lady Evangeline who had dragged Kitty away from him.

Evangeline was a frequent guest of Kitty's so she knew their house well. Before Kitty had known she was up the stairs and shut in her bedchamber.

"Charles and I have never been alone in a room together, let alone had the chance to discuss marriage!" she had exclaimed. "How could you have kept such information hidden from me? I thought I was your best friend!"

Kitty had rolled her eyes at the exasperated looking Evangeline. "You are, Eva," she had assured her. "It all happened so quickly. At first I loathed him, then that hate turned to admiration and the admiration transformed into love. Come to think of it, I really think I've loved him all this time. He is the most magnificent man I've ever known."

Evangeline had squealed with glee and she'd hugged her friend tightly. "Oh, my darling, I am so happy for you!" she'd cheered. "But alas, does he not depart Friday?"

Kitty had nodded. "Yes, this is why our impromptu nuptials are planned for Thursday morning." She'd smiled warmly at Evangeline. "Eva, will you be my maid of honour?"

Evangeline's hazel eyes had widened. "Are you sure?" she'd gasped. "Your sisters ..."

"My sisters will be bridesmaids also," Kitty had finished her sentence. "Eva, you are my best friend. Granted we've misbehaved together, but we've shared every secret and now I want you to be standing with me at my wedding as I will wish to stand beside you at yours."

Tears had filled Evangeline's eyes and she hugged Kitty once more. "Oh, I wish you a lifetime of happiness, my dear

Kitty. Is it possible that everything could work out so per-fectly for you?"

"I doubt it will be perfect, nothing is perfect, I'm sure there are tumultuous waters ahead but it is nothing we can't handle," Kitty had replied.

"But you won't be together," Evangeline had pointed out. "You will have one night and then he will be gone. Can you really be without your husband for that long?"

Kitty still didn't have an answer for that question. She had no idea how she was going to last without seeing William every day. She felt so safe with him, and with him being gone she didn't know how she was going to cope.

Kitty hadn't answered so Evangeline had pressed on with her next question. "What if he lies with another?" she'd asked. "Months without the company of his wife ... men get lonely. My mother pretends not to notice but my father has frequent visitors. And your husband will be in the Caribbean ... my, those women are beautiful and exotic, one could not blame him for keeping company with someone once he gets lonely."

Kitty had felt her heart take off. She hadn't considered any of the points that Evangeline had brought to her attention. It was not uncommon for married men to take a mistress. Her father was the exception, as well as her Uncle Daniel, but men like them were scarce. What if William betrayed her? "Eva," Kitty had whispered in a distressed tone. "He wouldn't do that to me, would he?"

Evangeline had gasped and clamped her hand over her mouth. "Oh, I should not have said a word. Kitty, forget everything I just said. I do not want to plant a seed of doubt in your head just days before your wedding."

But it had. Kitty fretted about the fear she had for two days. She'd made it so that she and William were never alone so he never had an opportunity to ask her what was the matter. She knew that the sooner she asked the question the sooner she knew that she would see the expression on his face that told her that he had 'friends' in the Caribbean.

"You do not seem like the type of woman who is happy to be getting married in the morning," Little J commented as she lounged on Kitty's bed as Kitty fixed the bodice on her emerald gown. Little J did not care if she creased her pale blue gown or the fact that her blonde curls were coming loose from the up – do that one of the maids had fixed for her.

Kitty did not know what to say to her sister so she chose to ignore her. Instead, she turned away from the mirror and shrugged her shoulders nervously. "Do I look alright?" she asked her sister.

Little J beamed. "You look beautiful as always, Kitty. I suspect the gentleman in attendance tonight will be very upset that you are off limits."

Kitty felt like saying that she wished women saw married men the same way but she didn't want to let anyone know what she was thinking. "Come along," she ushered her sister. "We are expected presently."

When they arrived at the ball, Kitty kept both her sister and her cousin at her sides, making sure the conversation never ceased so that William couldn't get her attention. She knew she was being ridiculous but fear overshadowed her logic at that moment.

The ballroom was not as immaculately decorated as society parties usually were; instead only blue velvet curtains were hung behind the orchestra to honour the departing heroes. The room was completely dotted with blue coats, both dancing and standing idly chatting to the young ladies. Kitty spotted Evangeline on the floor dancing with Charles and felt a sudden surge of resentment fill her. Why did Evangeline have to speak? She could have been blissfully unaware.

The orchestra were playing the quadrille already and Kitty was a little upset that she was missing her favourite dance. Many eyes met hers as she and her family were announcing into the room and she knew they weren't all congratulatory stares. She wished that she could have taken William's arm for comfort but she couldn't without inviting his questions.

The ladies were all handed dance cards which gave William all the opportunity he needed to take Kitty's arm. She jumped at the contact and cursed herself for feeling relieved in his presence.

"We need to talk," he said in a low, concerned tone. He quickly dragged her from the ballroom and out into the hallway. He searched for a secluded space before pulling her into the drawing room. Kitty could feel her heart facing. She felt as though it might beat right out of her chest.

He closed the door behind them and turned on her. His piercing blue eyes were searching her for any explanation.

"Are you having second thoughts?" he asked in disbelief. "Because if you are, then tell me now so that I may leave with a shred of dignity."

Kitty looked up at him feeling ashamed. "I'm not having second thoughts," she whispered. "It's just something that Evangeline said to me."

"What did she say?" William pressed. He crossed the room to where she was standing and took her hands in his. "Tell me now so that I may help."

"William," Kitty mumbled. "I know that I'm not always proper but I do love you very much and I promise I won't betray you when you're away."

William furrowed his eyebrows as he wrapped his arm around her waist to being her closer to him. "I know you won't, that's what marriage vows are for," he answered simply. "What brought this on?"

Kitty sighed. "It's just ... I know the women in the Caribbean are beautiful and exotic and different to the prissy English girls you're used to ..." she started before William interrupted her.

"Is that what you're worried about?" William demanded, sounding angry. "That I'll bed every exotic woman I meet?" he snapped, releasing her. "Do you really think I would dishonour my marriage vows and betray you?"

"I don't know!" Kitty exclaimed exasperatedly. "I don't know how marriage works! Not one of my friends is married and it's not like I'm going to go to mama for advice, that would just be humiliating and my sister is married to a clergyman so I'd like to imagine she is a nun in their home. I don't know what you expect of me," she admitted.

William folded his arms across his chest. "I expect faithfulness and loyalty," he said simply. "And what I expect of you, you will receive from me. I will remain faithful to you, Kitty, I wouldn't ever betray you."

Kitty's eyes filled with tears. "But you will be gone so long, Eva says that men get lonely," she pressed. "It's normal for married men to take a mistress."

A hiss escaped William's lips. "Do not speak as though you expect me to be an adulterer, Kitty, it's quite an insult," he snapped.

"I'm sorry," Kitty cried. She sat down on one of the settees in the drawing room and buried her face in her hands. "I'm a terrible person, I know."

She heard him sigh. She felt the settee sink a little as he sat down beside her. "I'm sorry, I should not have snapped at you, it just angered me that you thought I would betray you so easily." He pulled her close to him and she relaxed a little, as she did so often in his embrace. "Wherever you go I will go. Wherever you live I will live. Your people are my people and your God is my God. Wherever you die I will die and that is where I will be buried. May the Lord's worst punishment cone upon me if anything but death separates me from you," he whispered into her ear.

"Ruth 1:16?" Kitty smiled as she looked up at him.

"I may not have written the words, but I mean them," he promised. "You are to be my wife, and I unlike so many, believe that a wife should be cherished and honoured."

"How is that when you should be making me feel shame you make me feel as if I could fly?" Kitty sighed into his chest.

William rubbed her back soothingly. "I will never make you feel shame, my darling. If you wished it, I would make you wings."

Kitty blushed. "I should think you a poet, William, instead of a naval captain."

"I have not the talent for sonnets," he laughed lightly. "Commanding a ship is simpler than imagining the perfect words. If I had such a talent I would not have made you hate me so when we met."

"I am sorry," she apologised sincerely. "I was afraid of your answer should I have asked you directly of my fears. If I had not been so stupid we could have had two more days together."

"There is no need to apologise, Kitty. I don't want you to ever be afraid to ask or to tell me something," he replied. "I was afraid that you had changed your mind."

A smile spread across Kitty's face. "I could never change my mind," she promised. "There is one thing I fear though," she continued.

"What is it?"

"It would be foolish of me to ask you not to be gallant ... but you will come back to me, won't you, William?" she asked him vulnerably.

He leaned down and kissed her forehead. "Tomorrow night will not be the last night we spend together, Kitty," he promised.

She smiled contently. "Is it possible that everything could work out so perfectly? It almost seems too good to be true."

"Do not tempt fate," he scolded lightly. "But I can't agree with you more. It almost does seem too good to be true."

Kitty hoped it wasn't. She couldn't handle anything awful happening to her, her family or her soon to be husband. She remembered that if they were coming, his parents would arrive the next morning in time for the wedding. Perhaps what would go wrong would be the fact that his parents seriously disapproved of her. She was sure that was it. She would have in – laws that hated her. If that was the only thing that went wrong then she could handle that.

Chapter 14

"Kitty, wake up!" Little J hissed as she shook her sleeping sister.

Kitty groaned as she squinted into the darkness. She could barely make out the figure of her younger sister. "What are you doing?" she moaned. "It is still night time." She rolled over and closed her eyes once more.

"Get up," she ordered. "Mama and papa are already awake, James, Henry and your fiancée have already left the house and Mr and Mrs Aubrey just arrived!"

Kitty's eyes shot opened. "His parents?" she gasped. "What time is it?"

"Just after six," she replied. "But get up. They won't mind if you're hair is not perfect, they just want to meet you."

Kitty threw back her covers and climbed out of bed. It was then that it hit her. She was getting married in a matter of hours. Sunlight hit her eyes as Little J pulled back the drapes in her bedchamber. She was still wearing her nightgown and her hair was very curly as the rags had been untied. "Little J," she whispered. "I think I'm going to faint."

Little J raced over to Kitty and wrapped her arms around her. "Relax, Kitty," she said encouragingly. "You love this man, and he loves you, do not freak out and leave him."

Kitty's eyes widened. "I'm not going to abandon him," she said, alarmed. "I want this more than anything ... but I'm getting married in a few hours ... and his parents want to meet me," as she said it out loud she felt her heat beating faster and faster. "Why am I so nervous?"

Little J giggled. "It's perfectly natural," she assured her. "When you're in love, everything makes you nervous."

Kitty furrowed her eyebrows. "How would you know?" she asked.

Little J pursed her lips and looked a little uneasy. "I read about it ... in a book."

"Is there something you'd like to tell me, Little J?" Kitty said knowingly. Was her sister in love? Was that where she was going every day?

"No," she answered quickly.

Kitty was taken aback at a sudden realisation. "You are, aren't you?" she gasped. "That's where you go when you disappear every day! You go and visit a man ... Little J, are you his ... no, I can't even say the word." She stepped away from her sister and picked up her wrap and tied it around her waist. She could not believe that Little J was so intelligent yet so stupid.

"I do not visit a man every day, Kitty, and I am not a whore," she said, stumbling over the word. "I am as pure as you."

Kitty watched Little J's face for any sign of her lying. "Swear," she instructed. "Swear to God that you are not being used by any man."

"I swear to God that I am not being used by any man," she promised. "If something like that was happening to me you would be the first person I would tell. You're my sister, Kitty, I tell you everything."

"Not everything," Kitty retorted. She still was yet to inform her of where she escaped to every day.

Little J looked a little ashamed. "I will tell you, I promise. I just can't, not yet. It's not time, and I can't risk anyone finding out."

Kitty accepted that. She trusted Little J. She knew that when she was ready all would be known.

"Enough about me," she clapped her hands once. "This is your wedding day and you're about to meet your future in - laws. So let's get your hair fixed and go down stairs to meet them." Little J led Kitty over to her dresser and sat her down. She began untying the material rags in her hair and letting the perfect tendrils fall down her back.

"You're a good sister, Little J," Kitty smiled into the mirror, looking at her younger sister.

Little J looked up from Kitty's hair and smiled. "Not as good as you. You've always watched out for me. I'll never forget the time when you attacked little Robbie Redthrorn in Sunday school when he pulled my braid after I corrected his reading. Seeing his black eye for a few weeks in row reminded me that I didn't have to be ashamed of my intelligence."

Kitty remembered that day clearly. She'd never really paid attention in Sunday school but she did pay attention when Little J, the little five year old, corrected Robbie Redthorn's pronunciation of several words that Kitty herself had no idea how to pronounce. After the third time Robbie had turned around and tugged on Little J's blonde braid so hard that she fell off her chair. Kitty immediately stood up and punched him right in the nose. "You don't ever have to be ashamed of being clever, Little J. If anyone ever makes you feel like that then they will have to answer to me."

Kitty noticed Little J's eyes filling with tears. "I'm going to miss you so much," she said, her voice cracking.

Kitty smiled and stood up from her dress, her head still half filled with rags. She turned around and wrapped her arms around Little J's neck. "I'm not leaving just yet. William and I will find somewhere to live once he returns."

Little J sniffed as he blue eyes became glassy. "I know, but when you leave I'll be here with a house full of boys!"

"Who knows, perhaps you will be married before I leave?" she suggested.

Little J scoffed. "Who in their right mind would marry me? I'm a woman who believes in gender equality. All men want is a wife to give them children and entertainment."

"Hush," Kitty scolded. "You will find a man who loves every-thing about you."

"Like you have?"

Kitty nodded. "Well, I don't think he really liked my behav-iour when we first met and I can see why. I wasn't exactly giving the Alcott's a good name."

"You'll be really happy, Kitty. You and William are perfect," she smiled. "Now, let us get the rest of these rags out," she sniffed, wiping her eyes.

Within fifteen minutes, Little J had Kitty's hair out and curly, her cheeks pinched and her underclothes and a simple blue day dress laced on. Little J departed to her bedchamber to dress so Kitty was left by herself for a few minutes.

Standing at her window, Kitty watched as the sun rose. It was the last time she would be watching the sunrise as an unwed woman. She couldn't believe she'd been so fortunate. Many women married men whom their parents selected for them or because of the benefit of a title or a fortune and they didn't have the luxury of finding a man who would love them and be faithful to them.

"Sweetheart?" said Emilia as she knocked on the door.

Kitty turned around to see her mother walk into her bedchamber looking rather sad. "Yes, mama?"

"Don't you look beautiful?" she gushed as she crossed the room to her daughter. Emilia too wasn't properly dressed, only wearing a simple yellow day dress. Her golden hair was hanging down her back in neat waves.

Kitty found comfort in her mother's arms. She felt as if she was a child once more.

"I can't believe another one of my daughters is getting married. It seems as though it was only yesterday that you were five years old and preferred rolling around in the mud to acting proper - come to think of it, you still prefer other recreational activities to acting proper," Emilia laughed lightly. She looked back at her daughter and sighed happily. "I am so proud of you."

Kitty could feel her own eyes filling with tears. Her mother's brown eyes told her she was telling the truth. "Thank you, mama," Kitty said softly.

"I'm glad you're not leaving home just yet, I don't think I could bear to part with you," she laughed. "I've met Mr and Mrs Aubrey, they seem like fine people. His mama is a bit sceptical but his papa is a nice man."

Kitty knew that Mrs Aubrey was probably going to question her about her motives for marrying - what mother wouldn't? But she also knew there was another reason why her mother had visited her on her wedding day, she was going to explain what happens on the wedding night, something that Kitty did not want to hear.

"Now, I know you must be wondering what happens between a husband and wife the night of their wedding, so I'm going to tell you," Emilia began.

Kitty already knew what happened. She had a married sister and a friend who loved gossip. She'd also nearly been forced into it by a man who hadn't shown his face in town since. "Mama, that's really not necessary," she assured her.

Emilia smiled and nodded. "Alright," she sighed. She ran her fingers through Kitty's thick, dark hair before cupping her face. "Are you ready to meet Mr and Mrs Aubrey?" she asked.

Kitty nodded. "As I'll ever be," she replied. She took hold of her mother's hand and let Emilia lead her out of the room. They came to the landing where the sounds of voices coming from the drawing room became audible. As they walked down the stairs, Kitty asked in her softest voice "Will it hurt?" There were some things that only a mother's reassurance could quash.

Emilia squeezed her hand tightly. "Yes," she replied honestly. "But when you've got a husband who loves you, like William, he'll take care of you. He won't ever hurt you after tonight."

Kitty took a deep breath as she nodded. As they came to the drawing room Kitty could hear the distinct voices of two people she did not recognise. A footman opened the door for them and the men stood as Emilia and Kitty entered.

Her father and Sabine had been sitting on one settee and who she assumed to be Mr and Mrs Aubrey were sitting on the other settee.

"Mr Aubrey, Mrs Aubrey," her father said formally. "Allow me to introduce my eldest daughter, Lady Kitty Alcott."

William's father immediately came over to her with a warm and friendly smile on his face. He took her hand and kissed it lightly. "It's so lovely to meet you, my dear. My wife and I were thrilled to hear that our William was finally marrying." Kitty could believe that he was thrilled; his wife however did not look so.

It was as plain as day that John and Kathleen Aubrey were not William's biological parents. John was not as tall as William and was quite portly. His dark hair was streaked with grey and his green eyes were like little emeralds. His wife was similar to him in the way that she was not very tall. Her chestnut coloured hair was in a severe bun on top of her head and her grey eyes were quite reserved. She was quite thin and her skin was very good for her age but the scowl on her face made her look rather sour.

"It's nice to meet you too, William has said such wonderful things about both of you," she said politely, smiling at both him and his wife.

"That's quite interesting, milady, as we've never heard anything about you," Kathleen chimed in. She folded her arms across her chest and arched her eyebrows.

"It's been rather a quick courtship," Kitty said nervously.

"William's been our guest," Emilia informed Kathleen. "So he and Kitty have had quite a lot of time to get to know each other."

"Hmm." Kathleen looked Kitty up and down. It made her feel thoroughly self conscious considering she wasn't properly dressed. "Well, there's not much we can do about it now, is there?"

Kitty was taken aback. Had she just judged her based on two minutes of conversation? "Mrs Aubrey, might I have a word?" she asked sweetly.

She knew it would be completely rude of Kathleen to refuse to William's mother nodded. As they left the drawing room they ran into Little J who was bounding down the stairs in a very unladylike manner. Kitty knew it was just another element to add to Kathleen's already convincing disdain for her family.

"Little J," Kitty said in a warning tone.

Little J smiled kindly at Kathleen as she reached the bottom, not worrying about her sister's nervous stance. "Hello," she said in a friendly manner. "My name is Jane but everybody knows me as 'Little J'," she introduced herself in a relaxed manner.

Kathleen furrowed her eyebrows. "Why ever would they call you that?" she demanded to know.

Little J was taken aback by Kathleen's brazen question. "Well ... we have an aunt ... Jane. I'm named for her. It was quite ... confusing ... when I was younger ..." Little J stammered before Kitty cut in.

"It was too hard to differentiate between our Aunt Jane and Little J so she received the affectionate nickname that she has been known as since she was a toddler," Kitty said with a hint on angst in her voice. It was one thing to make your future daughter - in - law feel nervous but to verbally attack someone you've just met was out of line.

Little J shot her a thankful look before disappearing into the drawing room. The two women were alone.

"Say what you want to say, Mrs Aubrey," Kitty allowed her.

The woman's steel grey eyes narrowed. "Surely you can understand why I am confused, Lady Kitty."

Kitty nodded. "I can, but I don't understand why you feel the need to attack my sister so. She was only being friendly."

Kathleen nodded. "I did not mean for my question to come out so blunt, but I'd never heard of an Earl's daughter being referred with such an informal name."

"I love your son, Mrs Aubrey," Kitty said simply. "I'm so nervous right at this moment. Not only because in a few hours I will be getting married, but because I'm standing before my future mother - in - law and I feel as though she does not approve of me."

Kathleen pursed her lips. "I have not heard of you from my son before the letter we received the other day. My first thought, and I'll admit it, was that you were after his money."

Kitty furrowed her eyebrows. "I realise that William has money, Mrs Aubrey, but with all due respect, I have more. We love each other regardless of the money. I'd be happy if we lived in a shack in the middle of nowhere so long as he always came back to me."

Kathleen sighed and looked like she was thinking for a moment. "I think what worries me the most is that William is very ... devoted, I think that's the word I would use the most. He is very devoted to his men like I am sure he will be to you. I don't know your character, Lady Kitty, so I don't know if you're the type to reciprocate that devotion. Will you be true?"

That was something that Kitty could answer for sure. "Your son is the greatest man I have ever known, next to my father there is no - one more noble. I would never betray him," she promised.

Kathleen looked like she accepted her answer. For a moment, only a moment, her grey eyes softened. "I can see why he likes you, Lady Kitty. You are very fair and you speak very confidently. He is my only son, and I only want the best for him."

"Thank you," she smiled. She could feel her cheeks reddening a little.

"Will we expect you at Christmas?" Kathleen asked casually. "I understand that William will be absent but I'm sure we'd enjoy getting to know you a little better."

Kitty bit her lip, feeling awkward. "My grandmamma lives up in Yorkshire, it's actually an Alcott family tradition to gather at her farm and celebrate together. You see my Aunt Jane and Uncle Daniel, as well as Sabine, who you've met, and her two brothers, my family as well as my other sister and her husband all travel up to Yorkshire to stay with her. You'll be very welcome if you wanted to come."

Kathleen didn't look offended which Kitty was glad about. "I'm sure we shall visit that idea when the time comes."

"Do you approve of me?" Kitty asked vulnerably.

"I like how family orientated you are," Kathleen replied. "If you are like that with my son and my future grandchildren then I doubt we shall have any issues."

At that moment the door to the drawing room opened and her family and John all emerged chatting happily. Emilia caught Kitty's eyes. "Breakfast is served," she informed them. "Then we shall get you ready for the church."

Chapter 15

Her hair was pinned and curled into an intricate up - do. Simple white daisies, the kind she also would hold in her bouquet, were interwoven into her braids that made her truly look like a summer bride. Instead of wearing a bonnet, she opted for lace the matched the lace on her gown to be placed over her head as a veil.

Her face had been lightly powdered and so her skin was flawless. Her cheeks didn't require pinching as her nervous blush was showing through subtly.

At last but not least, her dress. There had not been time for a dressmaker to be summoned so Kitty had received her childhood wish. She'd always admired her mother's dress. It was outdated by about ten years but that did not both Kitty. The silk was so soft and the lace was so fine. The subtle pink ribbon that was sewn under the bust was Kitty's favourite part of the gown. While brides traditionally wore white it was just a hint of impropriety. It may not have been what her mother thought it was when she'd worn it but it was just a hint of Kitty's character that she loved.

Standing up from her dresser Kitty felt the layers of soft silk pass over her legs as it fell to the floor. She felt as though she was walking on a cloud. Kitty smoothed the gown over her hips as her family watched on.

Emilia's eyes were filling with tears as she watched her daughter wear her gown. "One cannot prepare themselves for the wedding of a child, it is simply too hard," she said, sounding like she was holding back violent sobs. "First Annie and now you, Little J you'd better not desert me!"

Little J laughed lightly as she put an arm around her mother. "I shall become a spinster, mama, do not fret."

Annie, who'd come from the church to the manor to help her sister dress, held onto Kitty's bedpost. She was dressed in her Sunday best, as was everyone, as there hadn't been any time to commission bridesmaid's gowns either. "You are truly the fairest of us all, Kitty. You will be the envy of every lady that attends," Annie said proudly.

Both Evangeline and Sabine nodded in agreement.

"I doubt it," Kitty replied. "Surely there will be gossiping women that whisper about my dress or my hair or the fact that the wedding happened so soon," she worried.

"And if they do then they shall have mama to answer to," Emilia assured her. "I will not tolerate any of my daughter's names being soiled. Anyone who besmirches you is lucky that grandmamma and Aunt Jane are absent as there would surely be a brawl in the middle of the pews."

Sabine giggled. "That definitely sounds like mama," she concurred.

"Alright," Emilia said, clapping her hands once. "Let us descend the stairs and put your father out of his misery. He is enduring two things he fears and hates most – waiting hours for the women in his life to get ready, and giving one of his daughters away at her wedding."

Sabine, Little J, Annie and Evangeline all filed out of the room in their fine gowns. Emilia helped Kitty with her lace veil as she made it cover her face. Kitty could still see perfectly as the lace was so fine. Her mother's brown eyes were kind as she smiled. "Are you nervous?" she asked she took Kitty's hand in hers.

Kitty could only nod.

"I am going to tell you what your grandmamma told me before I entered the church to marry your father. I will be forever grateful to her as it gave me all the courage I needed. My darling, you'll be great," she promised.

Kitty smiled, exhaling. "You were definitely great mama."

Emilia led Kitty from her bedchamber and out onto the landing. "One day you will tell your daughter the exact same thing. Marriage and motherhood, my dear, are not easy. There were times when all I wanted to do was throw a glass at your father's head and there were times that you children almost drove me completely mad but I wouldn't change a single second of it. I would not change anything in my life."

"Not even your first marriage?" Kitty wondered aloud.

Emilia shook her head. "Not even that. I'm a better person I think, because of it. I'm more resilient and compassionate. I bear scars but they don't define me anymore, just as your past does not define you," she said reassuringly. "You will be happy, my little Catherine, of that I'm sure."

"I won't be 'little Catherine' for much longer, mama, I'm to become Mrs Aubrey," Kitty said proudly. Her mother's statement was like magic. Perhaps they really were magical words that empowered whoever they were said to.

"Well then, allow me to be the last one to call you Lady Kitty Alcott," Emilia said proudly as they reached the bottom of the stairs. Her father was waiting for them with the widest smile on his face. Kitty could have sworn that he too had tears in his eyes.

"You look absolutely beautiful," her father said sincerely.

"Doesn't she?" her mother agreed.

"That dress brought down the aisle to me the one I hold most dear, I'd wager it a good luck charm for you," Sebastian commented. Kitty noticed her mother blush.

Her father offered her his arm which she gladly accepted. She still kept hold of her mother's hand and the three of them walked out to the carriage together. "I could not have parted with you, Kitty, to any less of a man then him. He may not have a title but he had true intentions. Title or not, that is all I want for you."

"Thank you, papa," Kitty smiled at him. "I am glad we are not taking a house straight away. I do need time to say goodbye to everyone."

"Papa is having one of the guest staterooms made up for you tonight so you'll be in your own hallway," her mother informed her as they were helped into the carriage by the footmen.

Sebastian grunted angrily. Clearly he was not thrilled about that part of his daughter getting married. "You are having one of the guest staterooms made up. I had no say in it," he mumbled.

"Oh, stop being such a spoil sport," Emilia rolled her eyes. "She is one and twenty, Sebastian, not eleven."

The ride to the church seemed like it only lasted seconds. When they arrived outside of the lovely building only her bridesmaids waited outside, the guests had already been seated. There were only a handful of friends that could come so the pews would be quite empty, but Kitty preferred it that way. She knew that once William returned they would have a grand affair that her grandmamma, her aunt and her uncle could all attend so she didn't mind so much that there were only twenty or so people inside.

Her father helped her from the carriage and her mother began to sort out the hem of her dress. Evangeline, Sabine, Annie and Little J all rushed over to be a part of it.

"He looks so nervous," Evangeline giggled as she handed Kitty her bouquet of daisies.

"Nervous?" Kitty repeated, alarmed. She hadn't factored in his nerves. What if he decided against it as soon as she entered the church and ran out the side door? "Nervous anxious or nervous excited?" she clarified.

"Kitty," Sabine said calmly. "All will be well," she promised. "He's not going anywhere."

"Alright," Sebastian said, clearing his throat. "Em, take your seat with the boys, bridesmaids, single file," he instructed. Emilia kissed Kitty's cheek before she disappeared into the church. Her bridesmaids all gave her encouraging smiles as they too made their way down the aisle.

She clung to her father's arm as they came to the doorway of the church. At that moment the organist began to play and she set her sights on the altar. There facing Joseph was her naval captain. Dressed finely in his blue coat, William's posture was rigid. Kitty could tell he was nervous. Standing beside him was a man dressed similarly to him, whom she assumed was his second in command. She'd heard his named mentioned a few times – Commander George Gates.

All eyes were on her as she and her father began to walk down the aisle. Several people whispered but others just smiled and stared. Kitty hoped that they were all thinking good thoughts.

The church was not decorated spectacularly. There was a fine piece of white fabric on the floor for the bridal party to walk down but that was it. She didn't mind though, material things weren't important.

When she reached the end of the aisle she felt the butter-flies in her stomach melt away. This was what she wanted, and there was no reason to be nervous.

Sebastian lifted the veil over her face and leaned down to kiss her on the cheek. His dark blue eyes were watery as she looked into them. "Thank you, papa," she whispered.

"I love you, Kitty," he replied.

It was then that she was able to stand beside William. He did not look down at her, he just kept looking straight ahead.

Kitty smiled as she leaned toward him ever so slightly. "You'll be great," she whispered.

At that moment he looked down at her and his eyes both widened and softened. His pursed lips relaxed and turned into a loving smile. "We'll be great," he countered.

Joseph cleared his throat to gather the attention of the church. "Dearly beloved, we are gathered here today to unite this man," he gestured to William. "And this woman," he gestured to Kitty. "In Holy matrimony," he finished. "I could preach about marriage for an hour but I'd wager you're all desperate to go back to Ethridge Manor and celebrate, as am I," Joseph grinned and the whole church laughed. Kitty herself giggled as Joseph was not usually invited to the wedding receptions, only usually asked to marry the couple and then be gone. "So, I say we get straight to the vows."

"I like him," William whispered to Kitty.

"He's a nice man, he puts you to sleep very easily, Sunday mass is the best sleep I ever get," Kitty whispered back with a cheeky smile on her face.

"William," Joseph said, interrupting their whispers. "Repeat after me," he instructed. "I, William," he began.

William turned to Kitty and took her hand, looking deep into her eyes. Kitty's butterflies immediately returned as he looked into her eyes. Those brilliant blue hues would be the ones she would wake up beside every day for the rest of her life. It made her all the more aware of what was to happen that night.

"I, William," he repeated.

"Take thee, Catherine."

"Take thee, Catherine."

"To be my lawful wedded wife."

"To be my lawful wedded wife," William said smiling.

"To have and to hold from this day forward," Joseph continued.

"To have and to hold from this day forward."

"For better for worse, for richer or poorer, in sickness and in health," Joseph recited from memory.

"For better for worse, for richer or poorer, in sickness and in health," William repeated.

"To love, cherish, and obey, till death us do part, according to God's holy ordinance; and thereto I plight thee my troth," Joseph finished.

"To love, cherish and obey, till death us do part, according to God's holy ordinance; and thereto I plight thee my troth," William took a deep breath. If it had been elsewhere, Kitty would have asked what 'troth' meant. She was not an imbecile, but some things were a little too old fashioned.

"Catherine, repeat after me," Joseph instructed. "I, Catherine."

"I, Catherine," she breathed. This was it, there was no ifs ands or buts now. It was just her and William till death would they part ... and of course one or two children.

"Take thee, William."

"Take thee, William." William smiled as she said his name. She could tell he was relieved to have his part over and done with.

"To be my lawful wedded husband."

"To be my lawful wedded husband." She smiled widely at the word 'husband'.

"To have and to hold from this day forward."

"To have and to hold from this day forward."

"For better for worse, for richer for poorer, in sickness and in health."

"For better for worse, for richer for poorer, in sickness and in health."

"To love, cherish, and to obey, till death us do part, according to God's holy ordinance; and thereto I give thee my troth."

"To love, cherish, and to obey, till death us do part, according to God's holy ordinance; and thereto I give thee my troth." Kitty sighed a breath of relief as she finished.

"Now for the ring," Joseph continued.

Commander Gates handed William the little golden circle that she would wear for the rest of her life.

"Place the ring on her finger and repeat after me," Joseph instructed.

William placed the ring on her ring finger and awaited Joseph's words.

"With this ring I thee wed, with my body I thee worship, and with all my worldly goods I thee endow: In the name of the Father, and of the Son and of the Holy Ghost, Amen."

"With this ring I thee wed, with my body I thee worship, and with all my worldly goods I thee endow: In the name of the Father, and of the Son and of the Holy Ghost, Amen." William squeezed her hand and then traced the golden ring with his index finger. It felt strange wearing it, but it was comforting at the same time.

"With the power vested in me, I now pronounce you husband and wife. You may kiss your bride, Captain," Joseph bowed his head and stepped back.

Kitty beamed as she stood up on her toes to meet William's lips. The church cheered and applauded. When they broke apart William's arm snaked its way around her waist, as he could do now that they were wed. She was a married woman. She was quite married and quite blissful.

"Mrs Aubrey," he whispered in her ear as they walked back down the aisle. "How do you feel?"

"Euphoric!" she exclaimed. "Positively euphoric!"

After a meal of French specialties that Mrs Norris had so beautifully prepared, three glasses of champagne and several hours of dancing, Kitty was lying on William's chest in the stateroom that had been prepared for them.

Kitty had been in the room several times before but it had never looked so grand. The linens had been replaced with pure white sheets with golden fringe. The canopy matched and had the luxury of a layer of the same white lace that Kitty had worn on her veil wrapped around each corner.

Several bouquets of flowers on every surface let off a fresh perfume and Kitty was very thankful to the three glasses of liquid courage that she had consumed.

She sighed happily as she played with one of his dark blonde chest hairs. "My whole life is in this moment," she whispered.

He ran his hands up and down her bare back lightly. "That gives me quite a lot to live up to for next time, you realise," he whispered back, leaning forward to kiss her forehead.

"In your vows, you promised to obey me, so when I give you an order, you'll have to follow it, alright?" Kitty instructed. She looked up at his peaceful blue eyes as he nodded in agreement.

"What is it that you ask of me?"

"As soon as you can, without a moments delay, you must promise to return home to me," she said seriously.

"And I have no say in the matter?" he asked, feigning offence.

"Absolutely none," she grinned, shaking her head.

"Then I shall have to oblige my wife," he sighed, laying his head back in the pillow. "How odious a task."

She playfully slapped his chest and crawled up to the pillow to lie beside him. "Will you write me when you arrive? And give me a return address. I don't want to be presumptuous but I may or may not have exciting news for you."

William knew exactly what she was talking about. His hand moved from her back to her flat and empty stomach. "I should love to receive that letter," he whispered excitedly. "How grand it would be to return to a child with your dark hair and your beautiful eyes. Such an interesting shade of blue they are, however they are not good at hiding your feelings, my darling, for that I am thankful."

"I'm glad you enjoy my flaws," she sighed.

"There are none," he replied as he cradled her face as he lay on his side. "It will be the hardest thing I'll ever face in my life – leaving you," he said honestly.

"Let it be the last time we must ever say goodbye," she replied.

William looked up to the grandfather clock in the corner of the room and sighed. "We have to be up in five hours," he said sadly. "Let us sleep; I want to know what it feels like to have my wife fall asleep in my arms."

Chapter 16

Kitty felt as if she could have been in mourning. She'd thought she'd prepared herself for goodbye but she was nowhere near ready. Her family and William's parents had gathered down at the dock, as had the wives and families of the other naval officers, to say goodbye.

The grey skies let off an ominous feelings and threatened rain. It did not feel like summer but it did feel like goodbye.

Docked next to the magnificent Royal Rose was the trade ship that flew the East India Trading Company flag. On board were all sorts of things from tea to weaponry. Kitty didn't know why it was so important to have a naval escort – what did it matter if a little tea was lost? But she knew that she wasn't about to change the King's decision, though if she had the opportunity she would give him a piece of her mind.

The thought of becoming a stowaway had crossed her mind but she knew it would only cause trouble.

William snapped her out of her trance by squeezing her hands in his. "Kitty?"

Her eyes flashed to his bright blue irises. They were filled with worry and concern. Why should he be worried and concerned about her? He was the one that was sailing into dangerous waters.

"Please don't go anywhere on your own," he instructed in a soft voice. "Married or not, you're still a beautiful woman and some men, namely an unmentionable man, have no qualms with violating you."

Kitty nodded, choosing to obey him. "I won't," she promised. "Will you do something for me?" she asked.

William nodded, bringing his hand to her cheek.

"Do not be a hero," she said sadly. "It may be horrid of me to ask as you are anything but a coward but you are sailing off with a hundred and twenty guns strapped to the walls of the ship."

William's face softened as he smiled slightly. "I've already told you I'm coming home. As soon as the trades are complete and we are free I'll be right back here by your side." He leaned forward and kissed her forehead. He then placed his hand on her flat stomach. "Take care of my son, won't you?" he whispered in her ear.

"How do you know it is a boy? And how do you even know I'm with child?" she arched one of her eyebrows.

"Wishful thinking, I suppose," he smiled.

At that moment there were cries aboard the Royal Rose which Kitty knew meant that they had to depart. William looked up onto the deck regretfully before returning to her.

"I will write you as soon as I can," he promised. "I can't promise that we'll be in one place for too long so I doubt I'll be able to give you a return address but I will give you a time frame in my letter."

"Captain," said a man standing behind Kitty. She turned around to see Commander Gates looking stern. He met her eyes and bowed his head. "Milady," he greeted formally.

"Commander," she smiled slightly.

"Is it time?" William asked his second in command regretfully.

"It is," Commander Gates nodded.

As if on cue, the clouds that threatened rain began to spill. She was thankful to the little wet droplets as they disguised her tears. Her family were standing twenty feet behind her all looking solemn.

Kitty pulled a letter from her person and handed it to him. He closed his hands over the paper to keep it safe from the rain.

"What's this?" he asked curiously.

"A letter, do not read it now or when you are on board or tomorrow even, just read it when you need to hear my voice, or my pathetic excuse for counsel," Kitty said bashfully. She immediately regretted giving him the letter, he probably thought her ridiculous.

Instead of scoffing or throwing the letter in the pools of water that were collecting on the docks he slipped it into his pocket. "I shall keep it safe until I need it." He leaned down and pressed his lips to hers. The kiss was soft and short, but it still made Kitty want to collapse on the ground wailing.

"I love you," she whispered.

"As I you," he replied. "I'll return before you know it."

"I'll hold you to your word," she said, forcing a smile onto her mouth. With that he turned away from her. With his

Commander they both walked up the ramp to the ship where the other officers saluted them. The ramp was removed and the anchor was pulled from the ocean. The young boys dressed in their best tweed scurried along the harbour untying the ropes that secured the ships to the harbour.

He appeared on deck as he smiled directly at Kitty one last time. Kitty couldn't help the menacing feeling she got in the pit of her stomach that told her it would be the last time she saw him.

The rain suddenly stopped hitting her face when a thick parasol shielded her. Instead of it being her mother or Little J, it was Kathleen Aubrey.

"Just wait, dear," she instructed, sounding almost kind. "In twenty minutes he won't be able to see you anymore and you can collapse in that fit of tears I know you're desperate to do."

The Royal Rose followed the East India Trading Company ship slowly as they departed. True as Kathleen had promised, after twenty minutes both ships had become far enough away that Kitty could let her knees give way.

But she refused to let them. She wouldn't cry, not there. Her worries were ridiculous, he'd promised to return and there were people far worse off in life than she was. It wouldn't be that long, a year at most, and what was a year?

Instead she watched. She watched until the Royal Rose and her companion disappeared from the horizon. She'd been standing so long that she'd lost the feeling in her legs. The rain had stopped yet it left her clothes cold and damp.

Kathleen still remained at her side and her family were now in the carriages just so they could have a seat. "With every departure, my dear, it gets easier," she promised. "I know it feels like he's so far away, that he's never going to return home but it's not true. My son and I have said goodbye a dozen times before so I know exactly how you feel, but know that he has returned to me every single time," she assured her. "However I feel this one will be the last. I doubt any future journeys will be torture for a husband like he, especially when he has a young, lovely wife at home."

Kitty peered at Kathleen curiously. "Are we friends, Mrs Aubrey?"

Kathleen's grey eyes softened. "We're both 'Mrs Aubrey' now, aren't we? We must stick together. Now come along. Your parents and siblings have waited in the rain long enough. We must all return to Ethridge and dry off. I expect a cup of tea and some hot soup are in order."

Kitty conceded and allowed Kathleen to lead her over to the carriages. Her mother immediately stepped out and enveloped Kitty in her arms. Her golden hair was quite wet but Emilia didn't seem to notice. "How are you, my darling?" she asked sadly. "Mrs Aubrey advised me that she was more suited to comforting you on this matter." Kitty did not miss the annoyed look her mother shot at Kathleen.

"Mrs Aubrey understands, mama," Kitty spoke truthfully. "Just as you understand for several other matters on which I need counsel."

Emilia kissed Kitty's forehead and pulled her into the carriage. "Thank you, Mrs Aubrey," Emilia smiled just as the carriage door closed.

"You'll be alright," her father promised just as Little J took her hand.

"I know," Kitty replied. A year was what she had to wait. A year would not be the death of her.

Two months passed. June rolled into July and July became August and before anyone knew it, it was nearly time for Sabine to return to Nottingham. In those two months Kathleen and John had returned to Kent with the promise that they too would join the Alcotts and the Winchesters at Grandmamma Catherine's farm for Christmas.

In those two months James had been released from Sebastian's side and had begun courting a young woman named Miss Sarah Smith who Emilia really disliked as she feared the woman only wished to be the next Countess and not James' wife.

In those two months Little J had not snuck out of the house once which gave Kitty the suspicion that she'd either separated from her lover or whatever she was doing had ceased.

In those two months Sabine had not stopped ranting every time she received a letter from her family over her fury at how the new Scottish stable hand was running things.

In those two months Kitty had not received any letters.

And in those two months Kitty had not gotten her monthly. William had had his wish granted; Kitty only wished she had a way of telling him.

The days were alright. She occupied herself with visiting Annie and Joseph, reading thanks to Little J's encouragement. She'd immersed herself in Victor Hugo's 'The Hunchback of Notre Dame', a new novel that her father had recently purchased. She'd been enjoying it until Mr Hugo had killed off Esmeralda and turned Quasimodo to dust. She'd abandoned reading after that and switched to helping out at the orphanage with Joseph and Annie. That she did enjoy. It saddened her to see all the children that didn't have parents or homes. But they were all so happy to see her every time she arrived.

The nights were the hardest. They were when she was completely alone. She'd moved from her bedchamber into the guest stateroom that she and William had shared. It felt like the first place they had lived together even if it was just for a night ... in her parent's house.

Before she knew it, it was eve of September. The day before Henry departed for his final year at Eton and Sabine returned home to, no doubt, end up in the town jail for attacking the new stable hand with a pitchfork.

"All I'm saying," Sabine ranted at her final dinner at Ethridge. "Is that if I wanted Puissant to be exercised like that I would have started it when she was foal. She's ten years old, she's perfect for my trail rides but for racing? The man belongs in an asylum, that's all I'm saying."

"Really?" James sniggered. Sabine had been talking about Puissant's exercise regime for ten minutes straight.

"I've heard that horse racing is the sport of tomorrow," Emilia commented, sipping her soup elegantly. "Perhaps this Mr McKenzie knows what he's doing. If he's sees potential in Puissant, then why shouldn't he train her?"

"Aunt Emilia, she's my horse!" Sabine protested. "I can't wait to go home tomorrow and give him a piece of my mind," she muttered.

"Does that mean you'll stop giving us a piece of your mind?" Henry asked comically.

Sabine's eyes narrowed as she threw the napkin from her lap across the table at Henry. In any other household, such an action would have been an abomination but all Sebastian, Emilia and the rest of the family did was laugh.

"We'll miss you, Sabine," Sebastian chuckled. "Though I feel as though your family will be disappointed that we didn't do better this summer season."

"You cannot be blamed, Uncle Sebastian, you aren't the one with a boring personality," Sabine shrugged.

"You aren't boring," Little J interjected.

"You just have very particular interests," Kitty concluded. "You won't find a man that can talk about the various conditions of tackle in London." Kitty then wondered how old Mr McKenzie was. If he was young, then at least he could annoy Sabine as a romantic prospect, though she couldn't see her Uncle Daniel allowing his only daughter to marry the stable hand. "By the way, I have some news," Kitty said nervously. She hadn't told a soul that she was expecting, not until she was positive.

She heard the sounds of spoons returning to their bowls and suddenly felt the entire room's eyes on her, including the footmen who were standing in the doorway.

"What is it?" her mother asked, sounding concerned. "Is it from Captain Aubrey? It is bad news?"

"No, mama, nothing bad," she assured her. "Actually it's very good news."

A smile spread across Emilia's face. "Are you?" she asked excitedly.

"I am," Kitty confirmed.

Emilia, Little J and Sabine all rose from their chairs cheering and clapping and offering words of congratulations. The men however looked bewildered and confused.

"What's going on?" Sebastian asked, furrowing his eyebrows. Kitty rolled her eyes at their cluelessness.

"Oh, really, Sebastian, you are oblivious sometimes. You are to be a grandpapa!" Emilia exclaimed.

Sebastian's dark blue eyes widened as his jaw dropped. He looked positively stunned.

Her brothers both grinned and commented on the fact that they were to be uncles.

Kitty placed a protective hand over her stomach as she was hugged and kissed by the members of her family. She zoned out of the chatter over the preparations that were to be made and just imagined a pretty pink baby ... a little pink baby with bright blue eyes that were just a little too big for its face.

But papa was not there, and she didn't know if it was fear talking or actuality.

Chapter 17

Even though it was December, wintertime in the Caribbean was surprisingly warm. William had been gone from England for nearly six months and he felt every aching day of it. He'd written Kitty several letters but he'd never had his foot on land long enough to find someone to send them for him.

The Royal Rose had been following the East India Trading Company for a long while. Every time they made port they picked up more cargo and set off again, dragging the Royal Rose with it.

It had been a very long six months. The company of his crew was getting rather tiresome. Not only were they getting rowdy at the lack of female company, they were irksome at the fact that the ale aboard the East India Trading Company ship was completely off limits. William was getting bored also. Not once had they run into any trouble. After six months he didn't see the point in one of His majesty's hundred and twenty gunners being wasted like it was. But it wasn't his decision to make.

He spent a lot of the nights just staring at the stars. Every time he caught a glimpse of Cassiopeia it reminded him of the little spitfire he'd met and fallen in love with.

As the sun rose on the twenty – first of December, William stood at the helm like he always did. There was something about the open sea that he liked. It was the smell and the sound, and the fact that one's lips always tasted of salt. He liked the idea of being able to spin the wheel and point the ship whichever way he liked and he would end up on a different continent.

He was tempted though, to just spin the wheel around to the right and head up north back to England. The sea couldn't hold a candle to the pull he felt toward Kitty. If he had to choose between them, then she would win.

The men weren't awake yet, which gave him that luxury of some peace and quiet. They were heading back to the Caribbean to deliver their final load of goods before the ships finally were able to return to England for any repairs that needed doing. The repairs would take weeks which meant that he would have weeks to spend with his wife and his new family before the mission with the East India Trading Company was finished.

He pulled the letter that Kitty had given him from his pocket. He hadn't let it out of his sight since he'd received it and he still hadn't found the right moment to read it. He'd been lonely a lot of times, but he didn't want to waste her words on a menial moment. He had to make it count.

Just as the sun rose a little higher, the sound of a cannon being fired filled the air. William's head snapped around and he found the source of the sound – a black ship that flew a black flag. They would be demons if they were not pirates.

The cannon had collided with the side of the East India Trading Company ship, blowing a hole in her side that had no doubt destroyed the several guns they had aboard.

"All hands on deck!" William bellowed as he turned the wheel to the left to place the Royal Rose between the pirate ship and the East India Trading Company ship.

Adrenaline coursed through William's veins as he raced down the stairs of the ship and opened the trap door between the lower and upper deck. His crew came streaming out as they readied the guns above and below deck. The sounds of cannons being loaded and lighted were not quick enough before the sounds of more cannons blasting through the air sounded.

The port side of the Royal Rose was immediately hit as she bowed down to the sea after the blow. William nearly lost his footing but kept himself upright by holding onto a rope and pulley.

"Captain," barked a Lieutenant. "Ready at your command, sir."

"Fire all!" William yelled to his men. "This is what you've been trained for. Do not let –" but before he could finish another waved of cannons began to hit the Royal Rose as the pirate ship edged closer and closer.

Wood splintered as more holes were created in the side of the Royal Rose. They retaliated with all sixty of the cannons on the port side of the ship being fired at once. The cannons that made the distance blew holes in the starboard side of the pirate ship.

William could hear the angry cries from the pirates as well as the pained ones from his men below deck that had been hit or caught in the debris. "Blast them!" he ordered. "I want their ship at the bottom of the sea!"

All William's hopes were quashed as soon as he saw split shot balls heading for the masts.

"Get the sails down now!" he yelled. "Load the split shots, I want their masts down!" William could see it happening before his eyes. They were firing as fast as possible but their cannons did not have the distance or the trajectory that the pirate ship did.

The East India Trading Company ship had turned away from the battle. William didn't know whether to curse the captain's cowardice or commend his sense in getting away from the battle.

No sooner had the sails been lowered did a split shot cannon hit the main mast. In one swift motion the grand piece of wood began to collapse. It was then that he saw it. Commander Gates was shouting orders. The noises surrounding the ship were loud and he hadn't heard the sound of the mast separating from the ships. The mast was falling; there was a death sentence on the Commander's shoulders.

As if he were moving in slow motion, William ran to his friend. With all his strength he pushed him, sending him flying through the air. Instead William now took Commander's Gates' position beneath the mast.

He did not feel its collision. All he saw as his sight disappeared was the smoke left behind by gunpowder and the remains of the Royal Rose crumbling. With his last ounce of strength, he reached into his pocket and felt the letter there. Knowing that at one point his wife's hand touched it brought comfort to him. With a small smile, he closed his eyes.

Christmas came and went and still Kitty had not heard anything from William. Spending time with her beloved grandmamma had helped distract her for a time but it still could not calm the little voice in her head that told her something had happened.

It was now late January and the Alcott's were on their way home. She sat in the carriage with her sisters and Joseph. The three of them were chatting happily but Kitty found more amusement in absently rubbing her swollen stomach and staring out the window. It was snowing. The perfect white dust coated every surface. She wondered, wherever he was, be it the Caribbean or elsewhere, if it was snowing where William was. Even if it wasn't snowing, she still looked at the stars like he liked to and hoped that he was doing so at the same time.

Being pregnant was not as glamorous as she had once thought. At least, the women she'd seen expecting made it look a lot easier. She'd spent the first few months being sick every morning and the next few wanting to eat the most obscure combinations of food. At the moment she absolutely devoured pickled eggs and jam. Then there was the fact that she looked incredibly thick around the face, hands and feet.

She hated that most of all. But inside of her was a little person. And in three short months she would be a mama.

"Kitty," Annie said worriedly, interrupting her thoughts. "Are you alright?"

Kitty looked away from the window and towards her sister. Annie too had just found out she was expecting, but she was only several weeks along. "Yes, I'm fine," she said, plastering on a false smile. She was not fine at all. If she were alone she would cry.

"How is the baby? Is she kicking?" Little J asked softly. She slowly reached out to touch Kitty's stomach.

"We do not know it is a girl," Kitty rolled her eyes. "Grand-mamma's reasons are old wives tales." Her Grandmamma had insisted that because she was carrying down low then she was birthing a girl. Kitty was not convinced, she was sure it was a boy. The way he kicked was the way a young boy with a hearty personality kicked.

"Kitty, are you really alright," Annie pressed. "We know it has been a long while since you've heard from William but I'm sure he's alright."

"How could you know?" Kitty snapped at her little sister. "Your husband is right there!" she exclaimed gesturing to Joseph who looked a little embarrassed. "Mine is in the middle of the ocean somewhere protecting a bloody trade ship from pirates!" She didn't care that she'd just used foul language, she was past caring.

"Kitty, you needn't lash out at Annie," Joseph said sadly. "She was only trying to be helpful."

Kitty sighed. "I know, sorry Annie," she apologised. "But none of you can understand."

The rest of the journey was made in silence or the smallest amount of small talk between her sisters and her brother – in – law. Kitty had returned her eyes to the window until they dropped and she fell asleep.

Within a few days she felt the familiar jostle of the London cobble streets underneath the carriage wheels. It wasn't snowing in London, but the air was gloomy and the rain was falling. She wrapped her travelling cloak around herself tighter instinctively.

Pulling up in front of Ethridge she felt a little relieved to be home. All she wanted to do was curl up in her own bed and go to sleep dreaming of William holding her like he had done on their wedding night.

"Home sweet home," Little J breathed as the doors to the carriages were opened. Footmen carrying dark parasols helped the passengers one by one from the carriages, shielding them from the rain. Kitty was taken third before Joseph. She made her way as quickly as she could, however not moving as fast as she didn't want to slip and hurt the baby.

Once inside, the butler, Mr Carter was taking the coats of the family members and hanging them up. When he arrived at her he smiled happily. "You'll never guess what arrived for you today, Lady Kitty," he said knowingly.

Kitty's eyes widened. "A letter?" she asked hopefully.

Mr Carter nodded. "Yes, the mail is in your father's study."

"A letter!" her mother exclaimed. "Oh, come Kitty, quickly," she hurried her. They both moved as quickly as they could to her father's study where sure enough a small stack of letters lay on the desk. Kitty quickly sifted through the several envelopes before she found the letter that had her name on it.

"Mama, look – Port Royal, Jamaica!" she said as she read the post mark. She quickly broke the seal using her fingers and unfolded the letter.

Dear Mrs Aubrey,

It is with deep sorrow and my sincerest condolences that I inform you of your husband's death on the morning of the 21st of December, 1832.

Our Captain perished saving my life and I would like you to know that his final act was heroic and his final thoughts were of you.

His body, as a Captain's should, lies at the bottom of the ocean with his vessel so he may not be returned to you.

The attack could not have been foreseen, Mrs Aubrey, and he did his best he could to protect his men.

He would not have wanted you to enter mourning, he would want you to move on and find another husband to take care of you.

I wish you and yours the best of health, and again I offer you my deepest sympathies.

Sincerely,

Commander George Gates

The letter slipped from Kitty's fingers and wafted to the floor. Emilia let out a cry of woe and screamed for Sebastian.

The feeling in her fingers and toes slowly started to disappear as she went into shock. Her legs gave way beneath her and she fell to her knees. Her mother cried out again and tried to lift her up but pregnant Kitty was too heavy.

A wave of nausea swept through Kitty as she vomited onto the floral carpet in her father's study. She shook off her mother's hands and fell to the floor lying on her side near the pool of sick. From where she was laying she could see the words 'his body, as a Captain's should, lies at the bottom of the ocean'. Reading that over and over just made her picture a cold and blue William. Nausea hit her again as she threw up once more.

"No," she whispered. "It can't be."

They'd had one night together. They'd barely even started. How was that fair? He was a good man; he didn't deserve to die at the hands of criminals. He was to be a father, and her baby was never to know him.

Slowly, as if someone was dragging a smouldering iron through her insides, she felt everything inside of her disappear. She felt as though she should have been at the bottom of the ocean as well.

"What the bloody hell happened?" she heard her father exclaim in an alarmed expression.

"Hush," her mother hissed. From her voice Kitty could tell she was crying. "William has been killed."

"Oh, my God," Sebastian gasped.

All of a sudden the floor beneath Kitty disappeared and she was in her father's arms. She felt her head fall to the side as she was carried out onto the landing. Her father carried her into her stateroom bedchamber and put her on the bed. Emilia put a dry towel in a bowl and poured the pitcher of water over it. She wringed the towel out and brought it over to Kitty and began to clean her mouth.

Kitty just lay on her side watching the rain from her window. She wondered how long it would take her to die if she lay completely still. She hoped not long.

Chapter 18

It killed Emilia. Every hour she watched her daughter suffer was an hour she suffered.

She'd watched her for two weeks just lie motionless on her bed watching the window absently. Every now and then they could convince her to have something to eat but she never managed more than an egg. She'd barely gotten any sleep and Emilia was very worried for her grandchild.

It was not a normal grieving process. Usually the widow or widower would have an opportunity to say goodbye at the funeral service and then spend time with their friends and acquaintances reminiscing, but all Kitty could do was imagine her husband at the bottom of the Caribbean sea somewhere and she would never see him again.

She'd written to Catherine asking advice on what to do when one loses a spouse and she had replied that she would be there as soon as she possibly can. She'd also written to Jane and Daniel informing them of the goings on and they had also promised to be in London as soon as possible.

Emilia sat in a chair in the corner of Kitty's room sipping at a cup of tea. The tea was supposed to be for Kitty but she had refused it. She barely acknowledged her presence in the room.

"Grandmamma's written," Emilia said softly. "She's coming to stay, as is Uncle Daniel and Aunt Jane, Sabine as well. They all worry for you my darling. Aunt Kassandra and Uncle Peter also send their love but they can't be away from their farm at the moment."

Kitty didn't respond. She just lay in the exact same position that she had been in for the past two weeks – on her side and staring.

Emilia placed the cup back on the tea plate and walked over to the side of the bed that Kitty was laying on. Her lack of sleep showed. There were bruise – like shadows underneath her dark blue eyes and her brown hair was flat and desperately needed washing. She would never tell her, but Kitty also desperately needed a bath as she had been in the same clothes since she had returned.

"Kitty," she said soothingly. "I know this is unimaginably painful and that none of us can understand what it is that you're going through, but you need to know we are here for you," she said, stroking her cheek softly. Her eyes just seemed to see straight through Emilia. "But it's not just you that you have to worry about; you also have that little child within you that need's its mama to care for it. William would want you to take care of your child." Emilia placed a hand on her daughter's swollen stomach. She thanked the Lord when she felt the baby kick. Two weeks with little food and sleep and it was still alright.

"I think what William would want is to be alive, mama," Kitty murmured emotionlessly. "Do not pretend to know his mind."

Emilia couldn't help but smile at the fact that her daughter had communicated with her. "I do not pretend to know his mind, darling, but I know for a fact that he would want his child and his wife safe. So I'm going to go downstairs and order a bath for you. I'll have Mrs Norris prepare some sandwiches and then we shall talk. I do not want to get cross with you, Kitty, but I'm looking out for the both of you."

Emilia stood up from beside the bed and left Kitty's room swiftly. On the landing she found one of the maids carrying fresh linen for the guests that were to arrive in a few days. "Could you have some sandwiches brought up for Lady Kitty please, and can you get the footmen to bring up a hot bath for her?"

The little maid nodded and curtseyed. "Yes, milady," she said softly. She continued onto one of the guest bedchambers before disappearing down the servant's staircase.

Emilia gathered up the skirt of her black mourning gown as she walked down the stairs. Wearing her mourning clothes felt appropriate. She did not detest it as she had the last time. Mourning Vincent felt unnatural. Mourning a good man and a brave naval hero was right.

"Ah, Em," said Sebastian as he emerged from the drawing room. "Any progress?" He had been just as worried about Kitty. Whenever Emilia wasn't in the room, Sebastian would sit with her and account to her the happenings of the day even if she wasn't listening.

"She spoke to me," she admitted quietly.

Sebastian's eyes, which were identical to the glassy ones of Kitty's, widened. "She spoke?" he repeated in disbelief. "What did she say?"

Emilia wrapped her arms around her husband's waist and laid her head against his chest. "It was more of a snide comment. I was telling her what William would want in regards to the baby and she basically told me not to be presumptuous." She couldn't imagine losing Sebastian. They'd had two and twenty years together and it would never be enough. She felt as though they had only married the day before. It was exactly what Kitty was feeling. She had barely been married and now she was a widow.

Sebastian pressed his lips to her forehead whilst rubbing her back soothingly. "She will know in time that we are only trying to help her. Shall I go and sit with her?"

Emilia shook her head. "I've ordered some sandwiches and a bath for her. Once it is ready I'll go and help her bathe."

"I received a letter from Henry today asking if he could come home and be with the family," Sebastian informed her.

"No, he's to stay put. He can't do anything here and the only thing he should be concentrating on is finishing his education," Emilia said firmly. "Where are the others?"

"Little J left like usual saying she was going to Annie's," Sebastian sighed.

Emilia rolled her eyes. If Little J weren't so intelligent she would be worried but she knew her daughter was not in any trouble. She was not one of those girls that go herself in compromising situations. One day, when she wasn't worrying about a million other things, she would sit her down and demand that she tell her what she was up to. "Did she take a chaperone?"

"No, she begged me to allow her to go alone," he sighed.

"You really need to learn how to say 'no' to the girls," she scolded.

"I know," he admitted. "But she just looks at me with those wide blue eyes and I give in. She's far too clever to get into any trouble anyway." Sebastian had the same reasoning as his wife.

"And James?" Emilia prompted.

"James is with Miss Sarah Smith. He's at luncheon with her family. They're all penny pinchers if you ask me," he grumbled.

"I don't like her either," Emilia concurred. "She fancies this house and his title far more than she fancies him. Should he ever find a girl who has absolutely no care for his title then I shall push for the marriage immediately."

Sebastian smiled coyly at his wife. "So you never fancied being the Countess once again when it came to marrying me?" he teased.

"Of course I did, darling, it was the only reason I even considered you," Emilia teased back. Then the guilt filled Emilia when she realised she was flirting with her husband when her daughter was above stairs hurting. "We should not be behaving this way," she said suddenly. "I will go and check on the sandwiches with Mrs Norris and you go and write to Henry telling him to stay at Eton," she instructed, quickly dashing down the hall and opening the concealed door that led into the narrow servant's staircases.

As she arrived at the kitchens she watched as Mrs Norris and her scullery maids were quickly chopping and beating and whisking as they prepared for the evening meals. Emilia had arrived just as the maid from upstairs had arrived from an opposing staircase.

"Mrs Norris," she said in her soft voice.

"What is it, Bertha, I'm quite busy," Mrs Norris replied. She had worked at Ethridge for some time, since before Emilia had entered it as a seventeen year old. She was no younger a young lady but she was experienced and had a unique hand when it came to cooking.

"Begging your pardon," Bertha apologised. "But her Ladyship has asked for some sandwiches to be prepared for Lady Kitty immediately."

Mrs Norris sighed. "That poor girl," she said sadly. "I know exactly how she feels. Losing your husband at such a young age can truly destroy you. But no amount of eating will ever fill the void. I was just lucky I had a talent to fall back on."

Emilia furrowed her brows. How could she have not known this about Mrs Norris? But of course, she was a 'Mrs' living in a house without a husband. She just presumed all senior members of staff were 'Mrs'.

"Alright, Anna, fetch me some bread from the larder," Mrs Norris instructed. "Sue, bring me a few of the boiled eggs and I'll make her some egg sandwiches." Bertha disappeared back up the servant's stairs and it was only the kitchen staff still in the room.

Emilia stepped out of the doorway and made herself known to the kitchen staff. Mrs Norris and the scullery maids all paused their work and curtseyed.

"Your Ladyship, had we known you were there we –" Mrs Norris started but Emilia interrupted her.

"Do not fret, Mrs Norris," Emilia said kindly. "You're not in any trouble, quite the opposite." Emilia picked up a boiled egg from the bowl that Sue had brought and cracked the shell. As she began peeling it, Mrs Norris, Sue and Anna all stared at her as if she was possessed.

"Milady, you don't have to do that," Sue said, offering to take over.

"It's quite alright, I don't' mind. I just wondered if I might have a word with you, Mrs Norris, about your husband."

Mrs Norris' brown eyes looked confused. She wiped her hands on her apron and picked up a knife to slice the bread. "What about him, milady?"

"I couldn't help but overhear that you'd lost him," Emilia said awkwardly.

Mrs Norris smiled sadly and nodded. "Yes, I did. About two years before you arrived here as a child," she recalled. "He was a stone mason, you see, and his lungs gave out on him. He was a decade and a half older than I was but I don't think age matters when it comes to love."

"My condolences," Emilia said sincerely. As she began peeling the second egg she asked an awkward question. "How did you get past it?"

"I didn't," she replied honestly. "Not really anyway. I still miss him and think of him daily. What Lady Kitty is going through ..." she sighed. "Right now she's in denial. She's thinking 'This isn't happening, not to him, not to me' and soon she'll move onto the crying and the screaming. I broke a lamp and a tea set. But then she'll start to have a greater grasp on what's happened. She'll learn to live with it and she'll learn to carry on. She'll have a hole in her heart for the rest of her life but it doesn't mean you can't go on living. And she's going to have a baby. I never got that with my husband. She's going to have a little piece of Captain Aubrey for the rest of her life."

Emilia didn't realise that tears were rolling down her cheeks. "I don't know how to help her," Emilia whispered. "She just lies there as if she's catatonic. I want to call the doctor but I'm afraid that they will diagnose her with melancholia and insist that she be sent to an asylum."

"Time is what it takes, milady, only time. She won't be like this forever. We all deal with death differently," Mrs Norris said as she picked up the eggs that Emilia had peeled and began to mash them.

"It's true, milady. When my brother died, caught the death, he did, one winter about four years ago, I cried for about a month. Then we learn to get past it," Anna added. The little blonde scullery maid handed Mrs Norris a jar of homemade Spanish mayonnaise.

Mrs Norris mixed the creamy condiment into the eggs and then began to spoon it onto the bread. "Lady Kitty will be fine, milady. With death comes life, and that could not be truer in her condition."

William blinked a few times to clear his blurry vision. The room he was in was not familiar. He was lying on a small, single bed with coarse sheets and an itchy woollen blanket. The walls surrounding him were all white yet the window was open. From it he could hear the sounds of the sea. He was on land but he had no idea where.

Beside him was a small table with a few books, his folded up naval uniform and on top was his letter from Kitty. He smiled. He was glad that it had been saved. As soon as the thought crossed his mind the memories of the wreckage came flooding back. How had he come to be on land when the last thing he remembered was being on a sinking ship? Where were his men? How many had been left to the sea?

"Ah!" he groaned as a sharp pain shot up his left leg. His knee felt as if it was on fire. As he went to pull the blanket back Commander Gates came into the room.

"I wouldn't do that if I were you," he said in a warning tone.

"Excuse me?" he snapped.

Even though he was older than William, the Commander's green eyes were wary. "I wouldn't take off your blanket just yet, sir, not until I explain what happened."

"How many were lost, Commander?" he demanded to know. If any had died then he would be a coward. It was a Captain's place to go down with the ship.

"Three, sir," Commander Gates said sadly. "Two cadets and a lieutenant."

William's heart sank. He was alive when three of his men were dead. "Then why am I here?" he growled. "You should have let me go down with the ship, it was only right!"

Commander Gates' lips pursed as he stood up straight. "Sir, you were alive when the Jamaican fishing boat came upon our wreck. Had you been dead we would have left you as we wouldn't have been able to do anything. But you weren't dead, you were alive. You saved my life, Captain Aubrey, so I saved yours."

The pain in William's knee grew worse as he sat there. There must have been some damage to it. "What happened to the pirates?" he sighed, sounding less angry.

"After the Rose was destroyed they went off after the East India ship. They had a good two hours lead on them so hopefully they made it to safety. We can't know until we get word. I've written a letter to the King informing him of the happenings; once he reads it I am sure he will request our immediate return to England. I don't know about you sir, but I need a break."

"Commander, what happened to me?" William asked. "My knee feels as if it's on fire."

The Commander's eyes saddened. "I will ask the doctor if he has something that can soothe the pain. I'm afraid that it is not good news, sir. When the mast fell, it landed on your left leg … the bones … they shattered. There was nothing they could do to save it."

William felt his heart pick up as he realised he could not feel his left foot. He looked down to the end of the bed and realised that there was only one elevation on the blanket and that was his right foot. He didn't care what the Commander said. He pulled back the blanket and stared at the emptiness where his left leg belonged. Below the knee was nothing. It was a bandaged stump. "So instead of leaving me to die with my men with my dignity you brought me back here to live my life as a cripple?" he snapped.

"I should think that you should be grateful!" the Commander gasped. "You are alive! You will return to your wife and still live a happy and healthy life."

"What life?" he spat. "What life will I have? Kitty will spend the rest of her life being my nurse. Not only have you condemned me to be an invalid you've condemned her too!" He leaned forward and placed his palm down on the bed where his leg would usually be. "This will ruin her life."

"At least you have one," Commander Gates retorted. "I have to write three letters to the families of those who died at sea. You still get to go home!"

"Four letters," William corrected. "You will write four letters."

"Four?" the Commander repeated.

"Yes, four," William nodded. He would not return home like this. He would not look Kitty in the eye with one leg and have her look at him with regret, with disappointment and shame. He could not see the resentment that would fill her pretty blue eyes when she saw what life she would be condemned to.

"But sir ..." Commander Gates began to protest before William cut him off.

"Better I die and she can live a full life with another then she be forced to live with a man she will grow to hate. It is what's best." William leaned over and picked up the letter that she had written for him. He so badly wanted to open it, but he knew if he read her words and heard her voice in his head then he would lose his nerve. "She deserves better than this life."

"Your wife loves you," Commander Gates said firmly. "She would not turn her back on you."

"I know she wouldn't," William agreed. "But it does not mean that she will not hate me and hate what life I have tied her to. If I am dead then she can go on living."

"What will you do?" Commander Gates asked. "If you are dead then you cannot go home."

"I will return to Kent for a short while when I am able and tell my parents to follow my plan. And then I don't know. Perhaps I will sail to the orient or join a freak show."

Commander Gates was not amused. "What about the navy? What am I to tell them? I cannot lie."

"Tell them the truth but ask them to keep my records confidential. I'm sure they will discharge me, honourable or not." William stared at his knee and wondered if the joint still worked. Would he be able to use his leg if he had a false one attached to him?

"Are you sure, sir?" Commander Gates checked.

"Yes, Kitty deserves more than me."

"Alright," he agreed. "There is a man here in Port Royal that is good with wood carving; he's offered to make you a leg when you're feeling ready for measurements. But for now get some rest. I'll let the doctor know you're awake and he shall give you something for the pain."

William just lay back on his pillow, covering himself back up with the bothersome blanket. He instinctively moved his right leg underneath it but could not do so easily with his stump. He would not be able to walk let alone work and support his wife. It was for the best that she thought he was dead. He was being honourable. He'd have to tell himself that every time he thought of her.

Chapter 19

It had been a month, or so Kitty had been told. She didn't notice the time passing. February brought rain and severe frost. The weather complimented her temperament perfectly.

Her grandmamma had arrived three days before followed by her Uncle Daniel, Aunt Jane and Sabine. Her cousins Philip and Louis, like her brother Henry, were both away at Eton.

She'd been a little more mobile. She'd been bathing regularly and permitting one decent meal a day to be delivered to her. She hadn't been hungry but she had to eat for the baby.

She hadn't been anything. She didn't know how she felt anymore. She just felt empty. She didn't know what to do or say to anyone. She didn't know whether she was supposed to go back to her normal routine whilst wearing mourning clothes or whether he was supposed to stay shut in her bedchamber and wallow for the rest of time. She liked the idea of the latter.

Kitty sat in her bed and rubbed her hands absently over her stomach. Every so often her baby would move and it let her know that she would not always be alone. She didn't know how she was going to be a mother when she felt the way she did. She would be entirely responsible for a little person and she could barely take care of herself.

"One day I'll tell you about your papa, little one," she said softly to her stomach. "I'll tell you how he saved a silly little girl and helped her become a woman."

How was it fair that she only got one night with her husband? Horrid married couples in London got years detesting each other. She only got one night in a loving and faithful marriage? What wrong had she done? Yes, she had flirted and teased but she had never lost her innocence. She had never ruined herself and she loved her family above anything. She was good.

William was the most honourable man she had ever met. He'd done everything to protect her. He'd done everything to protect anyone. He'd served in the navy and led a noble life. How was it fair that he died?

Of two things she was absolutely positive. One: she would never love again. Nor would she ever marry. She did not care what Commander Gates said, she would remain a widow for the rest of her life. Her grandmamma had been a widow for thirty years after all. Two: if her baby was a boy, he would be named for his father. 'William' was a good, strong name. It suited the man it had belonged to and it would suit her baby should he be a boy.

It struck her that she hadn't heard anything from William's parents. She would have thought that they would have visited or at least written. But then, she thought, they would be grieving too. They might want to do it by themselves.

There was a knock at Kitty's door and her grandmother entered slowly.

"Good afternoon, dear, how are you feeling?" she asked softly.

Kitty didn't know why they asked her this, the answer didn't change. So instead she answered "Fine."

Her grandmother did look pretty for her age. Her brown hair that was a similar colour to her own was streaked with silver but her skin was still lovely and smooth. Her hazel eyes were cautious yet kind as she edged closer to her grand-daughter. "Luncheon has just been served downstairs if you'd like to join us," she smiled slightly. "Nothing too fancy, just cold meats and cheeses."

She, like everyone else in the manor, was wearing black. Kitty was wearing her white nightdress though everyday her black gowns, gloves and bonnets were laid out for her.

"I'm not that peckish, grandmamma," Kitty replied emotionlessly.

"Would you like someone to bring you up something?" she proposed.

Kitty shook her head. "No, thank you, I'm still full from breakfast," she mumbled.

Catherine sat on the end of Kitty's bed carefully. "My dear, no matter how misinformed you think we all are, I do understand what you're going through. I went through it myself, after all."

Kitty's eyes shot to her grandmother's sharply. "With all due respect, grandmamma, you have no idea what I am going through. You had sixteen years with grandpapa, I barely had sixteen hours!" she exclaimed.

Catherine looked a little hurt but Kitty didn't notice. She knew her point was valid.

"Grandmamma, you had sixteen years and two children with grandpapa. You were by his side when he died and you stood by his grave as he was buried. I had one night with my husband and he was killed in the middle of the ocean where his body lies. Unless I miraculously grow fins I will never see him again." Kitty sniffed sadly and moved off of her bed. She walked over to her ceramic basin and poured some water in from the pitcher. As she was washing her face she felt her grandmamma's hands on her shoulders.

"I'm well aware of the fact that I had more time with my husband that you yours. But that does not dismiss the fact that I know how it feels to lose someone. I can tell you first and foremost that shutting yourself down does not help yourself or your children – whether they are born or not," Catherine said a little firmer.

Kitty looked down at her stomach and touched it softly. "I eat and I sleep, grandmamma, what more do you want of me?" she sighed, turning around.

Catherine's eyes softened. She reached out and touched her face. "I know that it feels as if that's all you can do. Believe me, that's all I did for a while. I'm ashamed to say that your father helped a lot with Jane in the beginning. But especially when you're growing a little one, you need to show him love and vitality, as well as sleep and sustenance."

"I can't grandmamma," she said sadly. "I don't know how to just go back to normal."

"We can't expect you to go back to normal. Things will never be normal. All we can do is to help you get through the pain. Time heals all wounds, not fully, but enough so that you feel like you can breathe again."

Kitty wished she could see that far into the future. She hoped that a time would come when she didn't feel so empty. She knew it would. Her grandmamma was alright after all this time. "Perhaps luncheon will be welcome," she smiled slightly. "I haven't been out of this room in quite some time."

Catherine smiled proudly. "Everyone will be so happy to see you. Now let me help you dress."

Kitty hadn't worn a dress made for her size in over a month. All of her black clothes did not fit.

"Do you know what?" Catherine asked. "I don't think anyone will mind if you're wearing nightclothes." She fetched a clean nightdress and helped Kitty into it and then helped her into a silk wrap. "We would all be more comfortable throughout the day if we were to wear nightclothes. I now envy you, my dear."

Kitty did feel fresher wearing clean nightclothes. She also did feel more comfortable. She would hate, once the baby was born, to go back to wearing a corset. She would not miss the feeling of not being confined.

Walking felt odd to her as she and Catherine ventured outside of her bedchamber. She hadn't walked further than her basin for weeks. She hadn't realised how much walking for her was now waddling. Her baby was due to be born in a matter of weeks so she was at her largest.

"Hold onto me, my dear," Catherine urged as they came to the stairs.

Kitty gulped as she took her grandmother's arm. She took one stair at a time and Catherine was ever so patient. With the ground floor foyer in sight Kitty felt a sense of pride that she'd made a step forward, not matter how small.

Her mother appeared from the dining room with the intention of going upstairs. She paused in shock when she was Kitty on the stairs with Catherine.

"Kitty!" she exclaimed, a large smiled spreading across her face. "Oh, darling, I'm so happy you've come downstairs!"

Kitty managed a small smile for her mother. "You can thank grandmamma," she replied quietly.

Emilia beamed at Catherine. "You were named after a wise woman, Kitty," she said simply.

"Don't I know it?" Kitty and Catherine reached the bottom of the stairs and Emilia quickly took Kitty's other arm. The two women led her to the dining room where her family were already sitting all casually conversing and eating.

To Kitty, the dining room appeared as though it was a sea of black. Every single person in the room was wearing black gowns and all the men were wearing black day suits with matching cravats. Kitty felt out of place wearing a white nightgown. If she hadn't been so rotund then should would have been wearing an entire black get up.

The men all stood up immediately. Their eyes widened at the fact that Kitty had joined them.

"Kitty," her father smiled, looking relieved. "I'm so glad you've joined us. We've all missed seeing your pretty face every day."

"Thank you, papa," Kitty replied, not knowing really what to say. She noticed her usual seat at the dining table was vacant. She didn't know whether they'd always kept it vacant or if they knew Catherine would be able to convince her to join them.

She sat down beside her mother and Little J. Sitting opposite her was James, Annie and Joseph. Down the other end of the table were her Aunt Jane and Uncle Daniel, Sabine and sitting at the other head was her grandmother like the matriarch she was.

On the table was a range of different meats and cheeses as well as fruit, wine and bread. It looked like a picnic lunch except they would be eating it at the table.

Everyone began to carry on eating without carrying on their conversations they had been having before she'd entered the room.

"Do not walk on eggshells around me, please," Kitty murmured. "Carry on as if I were not here." She reached out and pulled off a small bunch or grapes from the food platters and began popping them into her mouth slowly.

"Kitty," her Aunt Jane spoke up. "We do not want to pretend that you are not here, I think we're just trying to be supportive. It would be disrespectful of us to just carry on talking." Kitty had always admired her aunt. From the stories she'd heard about her aunt's youth, Kitty was certain she had inherited her spirit from her. She'd once aspired to be exactly like her – a wild child in her youth and the greatest wife and mother as she grew. Her future looked in doubt.

"I appreciate that you all have come so far to be with me, but you will not be helping by just sitting there silently. Please, just continue," Kitty urged. With that the hum of conversation returned to the room.

Kitty found that hearing her family talk and hearing the sounds of forks and knives against plates helped distract her, even if it was only for a little while. She decided to engage in a conversation after about twenty minutes.

"Sabine," she said, trying to sound confident.

Sabine's blue eyes found hers immediately. "Yes?"

"How are you finding the new stable hand?" she asked.

She could tell that Sabine did not want to answer truthfully. It wasn't because Sabine was a liar, she probably didn't want to burden Kitty with her complaints. "He is very knowledge-able. Papa made a very wise decision in hiring Mr McKenzie."

Kitty caught her father rolling his eyes. "Uncle Daniel doesn't seem to agree with your response, Sabine."

The many conversations ceased and the table was content in listening to Kitty speak.

"It is a rare day when we do not hear some complaint about Mr McKenzie," Daniel replied. "I would have thought that you would have gotten to know him by now. Hasn't he been teaching you to ride like a man?"

Kitty's eyebrows rose. Her proper cousin riding like a man? She would like to see that one day.

"I was perfectly content with the lessons, papa, however his insistence on using Scottish colloquialisms to describe me continue to irk me," Sabine sniffed. "I feel as if I am one of the dogs when he calls out 'lass'!" Sabine tried her best to imitate his accent but dismally failed.

The whole table erupted into a fit of laughter. Kitty found that against her will, she laughed too. It felt nice, laughing. It felt good to know that she could participate in familial things and have everything still be somewhat normal. For a short while, anyway, she forgot her pain.

William's leg had almost completely healed. The scar was a healthy pink colour and the pain in his knee was no longer so severe. The pain in his heart, however, was as strong and as present as ever.

The letter from Kitty sat on the table in his hospital bed taunting him. He'd had to physically pull his hand back on several occasions to stop himself from reading it.

It had been two months since the Rose had sunk which meant it was the end of February. The survivors had been informed of their Captain's plan and had all agreed to go along with it. They were to return to London to board a new ship and depart on another journey to the Orient. Commander Gates, like the good friend he was, had remained behind with him until he was able to board a passenger ship to England so that he could visit his parents.

The local man from Port Royal had come to him earlier in the week to measure him for a wooden leg. What William had been expecting when it came to a false leg was a post that he would limp around on. The man, named Jonas, however, had other plans. He'd measured the circumference of William's calves and ankles as well as the length of his foot to carve an exact replica of his right leg. Jonas had told him that he'd made many false legs before and then men who recovered best were the ones who still had their knees.

"They still have the movement of a normal leg," Jonas had told him. "You won't be able to run or move as normally or as quickly as you once did but you should be able walk."

William didn't buy anything until he saw the proof himself. How could a man with a false leg possibly walk?

"Sir," Commander Gates called as he entered William's recovery room.

William looked up as he sat on the edge of his bed. The doctor had informed him that it was important to stretch out his joints to maintain the circulation to his right leg and to the remains of his left leg.

His left leg just looked strange. The skin at the end of his leg was badly scarred though it was healing nicely. It was just a ... stump. He was still not used to it. One could not imagine how disheartening it was to wake up in the middle of the night with the need to relieve oneself and not be able to do it without either crawling or hopping.

"Yes, Commander?" William replied.

"I've booked us passage on a passenger ship that leave Port Royal in a fortnight. Jonas has informed me that the leg should be finished by then. He just has to source some leather and wool to construct the strap."

William did not know how he would be able to put all of his weight on just a piece of wood and walk as if it was a normal leg. He would be too conscious of the fact that it was false.

"Thank you, Commander, for staying here with me, I really appreciate it."

Commander Gates crossed his arms and raised his eyebrows. "I know of company that is much more pleasing to the eye," he said knowingly. The Commander didn't exactly approve of William's decision to appear dead to his wife. William knew it was wrong, but it was right it more ways. He was saving her from a life of having to be his nurse and caregiver. She would grow to resent him for it and be tied to a man she hated for the rest of her life. This way she would be able to marry again and live a full life, the life she deserved. The actual thought of Kitty finding another man made him feel physically ill.

"You know why I'm doing this, Commander," William sighed.

"I do, sir, but I know that you're wife would want to be by your side in your time of need. Should you not give her the chance and the respect to decide for herself?" Commander Gates challenged.

William shot the Commander a murderous look. "We may be friends, George, but I am still your commanding officer. You will not speak about my wife as if you know her mind!"

"With all due respect, sir, I should think I do know the mind of any wife that loves her husband. Can't you imagine how she must feel at this moment?"

William didn't want to think about Kitty in pain. "It will pass. She will meet another," he said more to himself than to the Commander.

"Really?" the Commander scoffed. As quick as a flash the letter on his bedside was in his hands. William leapt for it without any regard for the fact that he lacked a limb and went tumbling to the ground. The Commander didn't make any move to help him, quite the opposite. He took a few steps back and broke the seal on Kitty's letter. He cleared his throat and began to read. "My dear William," he began. "Now that really sounds like an uncaring wife, doesn't it?" he said cynically. "It is the night of our wedding. You've just told me to go to sleep but I'm afraid I can't. I can't sleep because I don't want to miss a minute of this, of being your wife and being allowed in your bed without it creating such a scandal. You might have told me that you snore also, but do not fret, I find it becoming."

The words killed him. The innocent words killed him. He could hear her voice in his head, he could see her excited little smile as she wrote the letter while watching him sleep. He could remember their wedding night. "Stop," he begged. He could feel the tears welling up in his eyes and he willed them not to come.

But Commander Gates would not stop. "I don't know what happens on the seas or what misfortunes, or indeed for-tunes, you may encounter but I want you to have this little piece of home with you when you most need it," he read on. "I think this is the time when you most need it, sir, a wise woman this one is." He continued reading. "I can't believe that only a short time ago I thought you a pompous, and I can say this because I am your wife, pig. You were everything I disliked in a man. Now those characteristics are the things

I do not think I could ever live without." Commander Gates chuckled. "She's got wit, I'll give her that."

William gave up trying to stand, he just sat there on the floor trying not to imagine his Kitty talking to him and speaking those words.

"And if I am, like you wish, with child, I hope our baby is exactly like you. He or she would be lucky to have a papa like you, and I should be a very proud mama bringing up a son or daughter like you." The Commander looked up. "She might be with child, sir, you never know. You could be missing out on your child's life. She wants him so to be like you. Would you like your son to be like the noble naval hero who lost his leg saving a lesser ranked man's life? Or would you like your son to grow up to be the man before me who lets his wife believe he is dead because he is afraid that she will reject him?"

"Stop!" William begged again. "I can't hear this! I can't hear her voice!" Flashes filled his mind. Those devious blue eyes, the tease in her smile, the blush of her cheeks, the sound of her voice when she said his name.

"I will not stop!" Commander Gates shouted. "You needn't worry about me while you are away, even though I know you will. You've changed me for the best. I think I used to abhor change, I now know that it can be for the better. You've just stirred, either it is the sound of my quill scratching across the paper or it is because of your snores but I should like to climb back in beside you and lay my head down on your chest and keep that memory until I can do it again when you return home. So, until then, know that I love you and that I'll be waiting for you. For forever and a day, your Kitty," he finished.

He looked up with angry eyes. "She's waiting for you, even if she believes your dead! You took vows, sir! In sickness and in health!"

"Until death do us part," William shot back. Tears had spilled from his eyes but he did not care. "As far as she's concerned I'm dead. She's better off without me!"

"She is if this behaviour persists," Commander Gates snapped. "All my naval career I've looked up to you sir. You've been the greatest of us all. You saved my life and so I saved yours. If you do not go back to your wife then you are not the man I thought you were. You say that she is better off without you and I feel as though I should agree with you. She wants her naval hero husband, with two legs or with one. If you insist on being this man," he said, gesturing to William's cowering person. "Then stay here. Mr Jonas will be finished with your leg soon. I suggest you use it to march right on over to Ethridge and correct this."

William loss all sense of superiority over Commander Gates. "What if she rejects me?" he asked softly.

"Then she's a disappointing woman and you're better off without her. But by the sounds of that letter, sir, I should think she will be glad to have you back in her arms, with four limbs or three," he answered simply.

The thought of seeing Kitty again brought him immense joy. But the thought of seeing a sneer on her face pained him more than anything. He could not know every corner of her mind. He could not know, even if she did not show it, that some small part of her would not resent him for being unable to support her properly.

"If she does not hate me for not being a proper man, then she will hate me for being deceitful," he admitted after a while.

"She loves you, sir, she'll forgive you. She might yell or throw a few things because you do deserve it, but she loves you," Commander Gates said simply.

William smiled at the wise man. "When we return, if I have any credit in the navy at all, I shall see that you are promoted to Captain so you can command your own ship. My praise should get you a Commodore rank if you're lucky."

Commander Gates smiled proudly. "I should appreciate that, sir," he said gratefully.

"A fortnight?" William raised his eyebrows.

"Yes, sir," he nodded.

"I shall call on my parents first, and then I shall return to Ethridge." William knew it was a very good chance that she would turn him out. That fear in the back of his mind refused to relent.

Chapter 20

A wave of pain flooded Kitty's body as the next contraction hit her. She was glad she would only be giving birth once, as she would not be able to handle the pain twice. Her baby had been prompt. Born at eight and a half months instead of nine months. It was March 12th, 1833.

Her mother sat behind her massaging her back and both her sisters held her hands. The doctor sat before her giving her instructions. Kitty was frustrated at Doctor Turner. He spoke as if he knew the pain she was going through.

"Oh, mama," Kitty wailed as another contraction twisted her insides.

"I know, darling, I experienced this five times," Emilia said, trying to sound soothing. "Doctor Turner, how much longer?" she asked desperately.

"Not long now, milady," Doctor Turner replied. "I can see a head!"

Kitty closed her eyes and pushed as hard as she could. The tears were streaming down her face. It was in this moment exactly that she missed William more than anything. Usually the father would be waiting outside the room waiting for the first cries of the baby. Her baby's father was at the bottom of the sea.

With all her might she pushed one last time and the sound of a baby's cries filled the room. A relieved smile came across her face as she relaxed back into her mother's arms.

"Oh my God!" Little J exclaimed.

Annie was quick to help the doctor wrap the baby. "It is a son, Kitty!" she beamed. "You have a son."

Kitty watched in euphoria as her son was placed in her arms. Wrapped in a white blanket, the little boy grizzled with his new lungs. He was so small. Smaller than a normal infant as he was born early. His face was red with birth and his dark hair was matted. "Hello," she whispered. Kitty felt an overwhelming surge of love for the little boy in her arms. No matter how broken she was, she had every reason to live because of him. He deserved a mother who could mask her pain and invest every ounce of love into him.

"Congratulations, Lady Kitty," Doctor Turner smiled at her as her covered her backup with a blanket. "Does he have a name?"

Kitty looked back at her mother. Emilia nodded as she climbed down from the bed. "Shall I tell your father that he is grandfather to little William Aubrey?"

"Yes," Kitty replied, looking back down to her son. "William Sebastian Aubrey is a good name, I think. I'll call him 'Will', we're fond of affectionate nicknames in this family."

"He looks like a Will," Little J said approvingly.

At that moment Will stopped his crying and opened his eyes. There they were, the same brilliant blue as his fathers.

It both hurt her and endeared her to see William looking out at her from their son's eyes. She was glad that in Will she would always see William.

"Look at those eyes," Annie marvelled. "It's as if William was actually here in the room."

"Hush, Annie," Little J hissed.

"No, it's alright," Kitty silenced them. "It is comforting to see him in there. William's not all gone." She gently rocked her baby instinctively. He made gurgling noises and closed his eyes once again, appearing to go to sleep in her arms.

"I'll go and let everyone know that Will has been born," Emilia said proudly as she disappeared from the bedchamber.

Both her sisters cooed over her baby. It made Kitty realise she had to tell them something. "He only has one parent now," she sighed. "Should anything happen to me I'd like to know you both would look after my son." She would not choose between her sisters. Godmothers had to be able to look after their godchild no matter what and both her sisters were capable of that.

"Kitty, don't think like that," Annie said sadly.

"Yes, you needn't worry, you'll be fine," Little J chimed in.

"But if something did happen," Kitty pressed. "You would both take care of him, wouldn't you?"

They both nodded sincerely. "What are sisters for?" Little J kissed Kitty's forehead.

"He's a handsome boy," Annie commented.

"He is," Kitty agreed.

"William would be very proud of you, Kitty," said her father at the door of her bedchamber. Kitty looked up to see him smiling at her proudly. He came into the room followed by her mother, James and the rest of her family. They all gathered around the bed to get a good look at the newest member of the Alcott family.

"Oh," Catherine gushed. "I am a great – grandmamma!"

"Congratulations, Kitty," Sabine said sincerely.

"Yes, many congratulations, Kitty, you will make a wonderful mother," her Uncle Daniel agreed. Jane just looked like she was about to cry.

Kitty returned her attention back to her newborn son. He was so perfect and pink. She really did think that William would be proud of her. She would be everything her own mother was to him. She wouldn't let him know if she was her hurting.

She would be perfect for him.

A month passed quickly. Kitty had spent every waking minute with baby Will. Even when he was sleeping she just liked watching him. He was her entire world. As the rain cleared and March turned into April. As her twenty – second birthday passed Kitty decided it was finally time to go and see John and Kathleen Aubrey.

She let it go and she let it go but enough was enough. They were both grieving. Now that Will was born it was definitely time for her to visit them.

She refused to have her new baby dressed in black even though she was. Dressing him in a white cotton suit and a woollen coat knitted for him but Catherine she was ready to travel.

Her family weren't pleased that she was travelling so soon after giving birth but she had it do it. She had regained her strength and she was up and about.

"Can't it wait until Will is a little older, Kitty?" her mother sighed as Kitty fastened the buckles on her trunk. Emilia rocked Will in her arms like she did most days. "The Aubrey's aren't expecting you and none of us want to miss too much of Will's infancy."

"He will still be an infant when we return, mama," Kitty said, smiling at her mother. "I won't be gone longer than three weeks. If my relationship with Kathleen has deteriorated I might be back sooner than that."

"I feel as though everyone is leaving me," Emilia pouted.

Many people had vacated Ethridge in the past two weeks. Catherine had left for York three days ago and the Winchester clan had gone the day after. Annie and Joseph were back at their house beside the church, James was back to attending Oxford and Little J was back to her usual disappearing routine. It was basically just Kitty, her papa and her mama in the house.

"Mama," Kitty rolled her eyes. "When was the last time you and papa were alone in the house?" she asked raising her eyebrows. "Probably before James and I were born, correct?"

"I suppose so," Emilia sighed. "But I like having you all around. I didn't have this when I was growing up. I didn't have people around me all the time, people that I cared about. I wanted the opposite for you five."

"Mama, we had that in spades," Kitty abandoned her trunk and went over to give her mother a hug, careful not to crush Will. "I could not have asked for a better childhood. You and papa were the best parents we could have asked for. You are what I aspire to be as a mother. But we're adults now. You need to take some time for yourself."

Emilia's brown eyes warmed. "I suppose you all have grown up, haven't you? When did that happen? A minute ago I was watching you and your brother fight over a frog and now I am sending you off to see your in – laws with your infant son? Lord, how old does that make me?"

Kitty rolled her eyes. "You do not look a day over five and twenty, mama," she assured her.

Kitty could tell her mother didn't believe her. "Come along then. I'll have one of the footmen collect your trunk. Your carriage is waiting, my dear."

Within the hour Kitty was in the carriage on her way to the Aubrey's home in Kent. As she sat in the carriage holding a sleeping Will she wondered what she was to do about Will's future. The obvious choice was Eton for his education. Her brother's had gone there, Henry was still attending. Her cousins and her uncle had all gone there so securing him a place was no issue, neither was the tuition. Her father had already set aside her dowry for Will's education and future considering William had never had the opportunity to take it. He then could go onto university and study whatever he liked. She wondered what William would have wanted for his son's future. Perhaps he would have had other plans for him. Maybe he might've wanted him taught by a governess.

Perhaps he would have wanted him reared specifically for a career in the navy. She couldn't know.

"Do you know what, my darling?" Kitty asked her sleeping son. "You can be anything you want to be. Although I will heavily advise against participating in any naval journey that requires you to venture into the Atlantic."

After a days riding, the carriage finally stopped. Kitty was dozing and the sudden stop of motion alerted her. She could smell the sea already. She looked out the window and saw that they were already at the seaside. She figured that with a fishing business that it would be convenient to live by the sea. She smiled, thinking William must've had a wonderful childhood. It was a treat for her as a child to be taken to the sea.

"This is where papa grew up," she whispered to her baby as the door to the carriage opened.

As she was helped down carefully while holding Will, she noticed another carriage outside the Aubrey's small home. It wasn't a fancy, privately owned one like her family's but one that someone would hire to take them on a journey.

"The Aubrey's are popular today, milady," the driver commented as he climbed down to tend the horses.

"Yes," Kitty said suspiciously. The driver of that carriage was wiping down his horses absently, and seemed to want to be left alone. She cuddled Will to her chest and made her way over to the door. The house was very quaint. It was made of brown brick and was surrounded by yellow grass. The windows were small and painted white and the roof had been tarnished by the weather. Opposite the house was the ocean. A small, somewhat private beach that had a man made dock built about thirty feet out into it. Tied to it were a few fishing boats. She could see several floating orange balls out on the sea which she presumed to be nets.

She took a deep breath before knocking on the door of the Aubrey's home. "You're going to meet grandmamma and grandpapa today, Will," she cooed. Will stirred and opened his big blue eyes. They stared at her with wonder, a look that made the breath in her throat catch.

After a few moments the door swung open and Kathleen stood before her with an alarmed expression. She looked fiercely angry which frightened Kitty. She looked down at the bundle in her arms and her grey eyes softened. "I should have written," she whispered. After a second her angry look returned and she ushered Kitty inside. "You could not have come at a better time, Lady Kitty," she murmured.

Kitty furrowed her eyebrows. "I don't understand, am I in trouble?" she asked as she was pulled through the little living room and into the dining room.

Kathleen released her once they were properly inside. Sitting at the driftwood table was John who wore the exact same expression as his wife. He was joined by one other.

She knew who it was before he turned around. His blond hair, his broad shoulders, and his rigid posture – it was her dead husband. He turned to see her slowly and that's when his bright blue eyes that mirrored her son's. He looked surprised and afraid to see her.

"Kathleen, take the baby," she instructed weakly.

William's eyes immediately flashed to Will and he gasped. Kathleen took Will from her arms which gave Kitty leave to faint. She let her legs buckle and her eyes go black.

Chapter 21

William was incredibly relieved when the passenger ship docked in London. A month of travelling without having captain's quarters was not a pleasant journey.

Commander Gates had been a lot more pleasant to be around once William had agreed to go back to Kitty, and he had been even more supportive in walking at the pace that William could with his false leg.

It was truly a marvel, William had never seen a false leg so perfectly carved. If his right leg had been made of wood, it would have looked identical to the wooden one that Jonas had so expertly made. As it fit perfectly, his clothes were still the right size. His left foot fit into his boot and to an oblivious man, he looked like someone with a slight limp, not a false limb.

It took him a few weeks aboard the ship to truly trust the leg. Putting his weight on it made him nervous but after he'd done it a few times he knew he could use it properly. It was attached to his thigh via a layer of sheep's wool for comfort and leather for strength and a brass buckle to tighten and loose it as he needed. The top of the wooden leg had been hollowed out to the right shape to fit his stump. William couldn't thank Jonas enough. He gave him double his fee but he felt that he still had not filled his debt. Jonas had just asked him to keep in contact and if he ever needed a new leg then he was available for hire.

As he and the Commander walked along the London dock, the same dock that he had gotten engaged to Kitty. It felt strange to be back on English soil. He hadn't been there in over ten months. His wife was only a short carriage ride away. But he couldn't see her first, he had to see his parents, as when he returned to London, he was never leaving.

"I suppose this is where we say 'goodbye'," the Commander said as they reached the dock's end. There were several drivers standing idly beside their carriages that were for hire. William would be heading there first.

"You have shown me great loyalty these past few months, Commander," William said truthfully. "You've shown me courage and leadership ... all the qualities that a future Admiral of the Fleet must possess."

Commander Gates' eyes widened. "Admiral of the Fleet?" he repeated in disbelief. "You can really see that for me?"

William nodded. "My influence will get you 'Captain', maybe even 'Commodore', but you will make 'Admiral of the Fleet' on your own, mark my words."

Commander Gates' posture stiffened formally. "Thank you, sir. It has been a privilege serving under you," he said, saluting William.

"And I you," William saluted his friend. "And from now on, I am 'William' to you. I will no longer be your commanding officer."

"You will always be my commanding officer, sir," Commander Gates replied. "I hope I will be seeing you soon, Captain Aubrey, with your wife by your side."

William wasn't so sure. "I hope so, too," he sighed. "Farewell," he smiled at him.

They parted ways and William headed over to the carriages. He selected the one of the far left as the driver looked the most private and would be the least likely to start a conversation with him.

"Hello, there," William said to the driver. He was an older man of about fifty. His sour expression matched his dull grey eyes. "How far is your perimeter for passengers?"

"If they've got the money, I've got no perimeter," he mumbled.

William pulled five pounds from his pocket and held it out to him. The man's eyes widened as he secured the paper eagerly. "I need to get to Kent," he instructed. "And I will require you to wait for me to finish my business there and then return me to London."

"Five pounds just for Kent?" the man asked in disbelief.

"Is the sum not sufficient?" William thought five pounds was more than enough. It was probably what this man made in a month.

"For five pounds I'd drive you to bloody France across the Channel," he scoffed. "I'm Charlie, by the way, sir, climb aboard," he said, gesturing to the carriage. He took hold of William bag and put it up on top of the carriage.

"William," he replied. William climbed inside the carriage, giving Charlie the exact location of his parent's house and closed the door behind him. The inside of the carriage was not like the fine carriages that the Alcott's owned, it was instead made of wood with a thin, cushioned seat.

He turned on his side as he felt Charlie whip the horses into motion. He took off his boot and rolled up the leg on his slacks. Seeing the wooden leg still troubled him from time to time, even though it was better than having no leg at all. He unbuckled the leg and pulled it off. Jonas had told him that it was important to let his leg breathe. He thanked God that the leg was sanded smooth, if it wasn't he would have had nasty splinters.

He closed the thin curtain that hung over the window and blackened the small carriage. He wanted to sleep before he arrived at his parent's house. There was too much going on in his mind that consciousness was unbearable.

The sudden stop of motion roused him from his sleep. He moved the curtain from the window and smiled slightly when he saw the familiar beach that he had grown up on. His father's fishing boats were moored to the dock just like they always were.

Before he had time to collect his thoughts, the door to the carriage opened abruptly and Charlie was standing before him. As he reached for the small steps he noticed William's leg. A look of alarm and disgust crossed his face. "Jesus," he swore. "What happened to you?"

That was exactly the reaction that he was afraid of, especially if it came from Kitty. Except the fear stemmed from how he figured the conversation would end – with her little golden wedding ring at his feet ... or foot now.

He hurriedly reattached his leg and pulled his slacks back down to their usual length. He then slipped on his boot before climbing from the carriage. "I don't need a driver to ask me questions, Charlie," William snapped angrily. "How about you wipe the horses down and take my five pounds into town to the tavern?" he suggested. He was serious about the horses. The chestnut stallions were covered in a shiny coat of sweat.

William accepted his bag from him and limped over to his parent's seaside cottage. He knocked on the door quickly and it wasn't long before his mother answered the door. The small, grey eyed woman beamed at him and threw her arms around his neck. "Oh, my darling!" she exclaimed. "We were not expecting you!" she pulled back and looked around him. "But where is Kitty?" she asked, furrowing her eyebrows.

Clearly his parents had not received the letter that Commander Gates had sent to Kitty. Thinking about his plan now, he knew it would never have worked. There were too many holes, both literal and moral. "That is what I came here to discuss with you, mama," he said seriously. "Is papa home?"

Kathleen nodded, looking concerned. "Yes, he's having tea in the dining room – we both are. Whatever is the matter, William, you're frightening me. Is Kitty alright? Is it the child?" she panicked.

"What child?" he asked. Did he have a child?

"Have you not seen Kitty?" she asked, confused.

"No, after I'm finished here I'm to go to her … mama, what child?" he pressed.

Kathleen pursed her lips. "It's not really my place …"

"Mama," William groaned.

She sighed. "You are to be a father. Soon I should think. She was quite rotund at Christmastime."

William was in shock. A wave of happiness filled him. He was to be a father. He and Kitty were to be parents. He now knew that his plan was to be abandoned. He would not miss out on the life of his child, not for a minute.

Kathleen led him through to the dining room where his father was sitting. John grinned as soon as he saw his son and pulled him into a tight hug. "It's good to see you, son," he said happily.

William knew that his parents would not appear so proud when they knew what he had done. "It's good to see you too, papa," he replied.

Kathleen fluttered into the adjoining kitchen and fetched another china teacup. She brought it back to the driftwood table that his father had constructed and poured him a cup. "Sit, sit," she instructed. "Tell us what's happened."

William limped around the table to the vacant chair. Both his parents suddenly noticed his obscure walking pattern.

"William, what happened to your leg?" Kathleen asked worriedly.

His parent's reactions would give him an idea on how Kitty would react. "That's what happened to me, mama," he sighed. He pulled the chair out and sat down at the table. He accepted his cup of tea from his mother and welcomed the warm drink. "There was an accident," he began. "We were protecting an East India ship that came under attack by a gang of pirates."

Kathleen's alarmed look worsened. "I hope you strung all those fiends up. Come to the think of it, the gallows are too good for people who rape and murder – is quartering still a punishment?"

"We didn't defeat them, mama," William said regretfully. "The chain cannons came too quickly for us and the Rose went down. The East India ship escaped and the pirate ship went after it once the Rose was in splinters. I was unconscious for most of it ..."

"Unconscious?" his father repeated. "You're the finest that navy's got. Why were you unconscious?"

William sensed the disappointment in his father's tone. Clearly his son being defeated in a fight was not an honourable thing. That annoyed him. "I was commanding the guns, instructing the men, when I saw my second in command, Commander George Gates underneath the falling mast. I just ran. I pushed him out of the way and the mast took me down instead."

Kathleen clapped her hands over her mouth. "The mast fell on you?" she whispered.

William nodded. "Yes ... my leg to be more specific." He touched his wooden leg self – consciously.

"Why can't you just not be brave, darling?" his mother sighed.

"Mama," William said in a warning tone. "It was my duty and my privilege to save my Commander."

"How long until it mends?" his father asked. "Have the navy given you a leave of absence?"

William realised that it was going to be harder than he thought to tell his parents his wrongdoings. "My leg will never men, papa," he said honestly. "The mast shattered my bones beyond repair. The doctor in Port Royal ... he was forced to remove it."

A yelp escaped from Kathleen's mouth and John just appeared as if he was in pure shock.

"My leg is false," he said simply. "There's no changing it, I must live as a cripple for the rest of my life."

Kathleen burst into tears and John just sat there silently. The reaction, William thought, was just what he feared. Kitty was sure to leave him. If she did, then he still might be able to have a relationship with his son or daughter.

"Why are you so upset, mama," William said sourly. "It's not as if your leg was severed."

Kathleen's steel grey eyes flashed to his immediately. She looked angry at his comment. "How dare you say such a thing?" she snapped. "It may as well have been my leg that was severed. You are my son, William, so don't you ever doubt a mother's love. I would rather it have been my leg than yours!"

"Sorry, mama," he apologised quietly.

"What happened after that?" his father pressed on.

It was now or never. "I was in a dark place when I woke up. I was without a limb ... I felt like I was not a man anymore. I thought ... I still fear that Kitty will turn her back on me when she finds out. But when I was in the hospital I was convinced that she would be better off without me. I was convinced that she would be happier thinking I was dead and marrying someone else than having a cripple for a husband. I didn't want to turn her into a nurse. I didn't want to ruin her life. She still deserves better."

"You didn't," Kathleen whispered, looking frightened at the upcoming answer.

"He did, Kathleen," his father concluded. "You sent her a death notice."

"I thought it best," William said quietly. "I thought she could move on and forget me."

"And what did you plan on doing with the rest of your life? Abandon the navy and live in Jamaica?" John exclaimed. "What of your child?"

"I don't know, I wasn't thinking clearly," he replied exasperatedly. "All I knew is I had a young and beautiful wife that was tied to a one legged man. I didn't know of my child's existence obviously."

"How could you just abandon her?" Kathleen asked angrily. "I did not think much of her in the beginning but Kitty is a good girl – she loves you! She would not turn her back on you!"

At that moment the three of them heard a knock on the front door.

"How many visitors are to expect today?" Kathleen asked herself as she left the dining room to go and answer it.

"You will go back to her, William," his father instructed. "You will not abandon her."

"I'm not going to, papa, I'm going to give her the choice," he replied.

"You could not have come at a better time, Lady Kitty," his mother said from the front room.

William froze in his chair. She was here. She was in the next room! "I don't understand, am I in trouble?" Kitty asked. He'd missed her beautiful, soothing voice. He could hear her and his mother coming into the room. The sounds of their shoes on the stone floor let him know that she was standing right behind him.

He turned around slowly and saw his wife for the first time in ten months. There she stood. Her dark hair was encased in a black satin bonnet. Her thin frame was covered in a black mourning dress and her perfect skin was completely white. Her dark blue eyes widened and her pink lips parted.

"Kathleen, take the baby," she instructed weakly.

William gasped as he saw the small infant, bundled in white who lay sleeping in her arms. His mother immediately took the baby from her arms. Once she was parted from him or her, her knees buckled and she fainted.

William leapt from the table and caught her head before she hit the floor. "Kitty," he shook her gently but she didn't stir. "She's out cold," he said in a panicked tone and looked up to his mother for help. Kathleen, who was rocking her grandchild, pursed her lips. "Carry her into our bedroom and put her on the bed. She'll wake up in a moment, she's only fainted. Feel free to blame yourself."

William shot his mother a murderous look. She could hate him all she wanted, but she would not hate him when his wife lay unconscious on the floor. He hooked an arm underneath her legs and an arm around her torso. He had to trust his false leg at the moment as there was no way he was dropping her. He stood up carefully and limped down the narrow hallway to his parent's bedroom. He was glad that they lived in a one storey house. He would not have been able to handle stairs.

He laid Kitty down on the bed and removed her bonnet, untying the satin ribbon from underneath her chin. He could see the sadness on her face, even when she was unconscious. Underneath her eyes were deep, bruise – like shadows that told him of the lack of sleep she had been getting. She was mourning him. He knelt beside the bed and picked up her left hand. He kissed his ring on her finger and prayed it would still remain there after he'd told her everything.

Kitty's dark blue eyes fluttered open at the contact. She frowned at him and then smiled after a moment. "I'm dreaming," she sighed in a happy voice. "I like this dream. Don't wake me up, William, not yet. Just stay with me for a while."

He didn't know whether to feel touched or guilty that she had been thinking of him. "I'll stay with you for as long as you'll have me," he answered simply. "Kitty, you're not sleeping, you're awake. I'm here and I'm alive."

Kitty furrowed her brows and squinted. She pinched her forearm a few times and looked at him again. A smile spread across her face and she launched at him. In a matter of seconds she was lying on top of him on the floor of his parent's bedroom planting kisses all over his face. "You're here!" she exclaimed between kisses. "How can that be? I got a letter from Commander Gates … he must have been misinformed … but you're alive!" she leaned down and pressed her lips to his hard. William so desperately wanted to enjoy the familiarity with his wife but he couldn't do it dishonestly.

"Kitty," he said seriously, holding her back from kissing him again. "Commander Gates wasn't misinformed."

Kitty looked confused. "Wh ... what?"

"Commander Gates wasn't misinformed Kitty," he repeated.

She climbed off of him and stood up. "Yes, he was. He was informed that you had been killed and you haven't been killed, ergo, he was misinformed." She wasn't sounding confused anymore, she sounded suspicious. Her dark blue eyes were questioning him.

"You might want to sit down, I don't want you to faint again," William said worriedly.

"I think I'd rather stand," Kitty said sharply. She was trying to control the situation as best she could. He could tell she was panicking.

William decided that he should stand as well. He bent his left knee and held the false leg as he used his strong leg to stand. He could tell that it looked strange.

"What are you doing?" Kitty demanded to know. "What is wrong? Just tell me what is going on, please."

Once he was standing he took a deep breath. "There was an accident," he began. "Rather an attack that caused an accident."

"A pirate attack?" she asked.

"Yes," he replied. He figured that the letter had probably said as much. "They fired chain cannons on us and the main mast came down. I pushed Commander Gates out of the way and it fell on me."

Kitty's eyes watered and she nodded. She closed the distance between them and wrapped her arms around his waist. "I understand now," she said, inhaling his scent which he was sure wasn't that pleasant considering he'd been on a passenger ship for a month.

"What do you understand?" he asked.

"Commander Gates jumped to conclusions," she informed him. "He sent the letter before he had confirmed that you had been killed. It's alright, I'm not angry with him. I'm just glad to have you back, I never thought I would see you again."

"Kitty, that's not what happened," William said regretfully. He could have left it at that and had his wife and child back but he couldn't.

Kitty pulled back, her questioning eyes returning. "What do you mean?"

"When the mast fell on me in crushed all the bones in my left leg," he explained. This was it. Any minute now she would be throwing her wedding ring at his head. "The doctor had to remove it."

Kitty's eyes widened and a frightened expression crossed her face as she looked down at his legs. She knelt down ever so slowly and brought her small hands to her left leg. She pulled his slacks up from inside his boot and brought them to his knee. The end of his stump and the beginning of the wooden leg was visible.

He watched her face intently. She didn't look disgusted, far from it, she just looked confused.

She touched the wooden leg softly before looking up at him. "So you thought that by dying you were doing me a favour?" she asked emotionlessly.

Did she actually understand? Such a reaction was not one he thought would have come from her ... she understood. "I thought you would be better off without me. I didn't want to condemn you to being my nurse for the rest of your life. You would be miserable. You wouldn't want a husband with one leg. You would resent me."

Kitty fixed the leg of his slacks and then rose from the floor. She looked at him with blank eyes. "So ... you made up my mind for me?" she raised her eyebrows. "You decided for me."

"It wasn't like that, Kitty," William tried but Kitty interrupted.

"No, it was exactly like that," she snapped, showing her bubbling anger. "You decided to remove yourself from my life and push me into a pit of despair. You decided to pretend to die because an accident happened. You decided that I loved you so little that I would turn my back on you because of a lost limb. You decided to leave me. And you know what kills me? You made this decision so easily!" She was yelling now, she was furious.

He was an imbecile. He knew it clearly now. He could feel his insides sinking as he knew he'd lost her.

"Kitty, I'm sorry," he begged. "I thought you'd resent me for making you my nurse. I honestly thought I was doing the right thing!"

A hiss escaped her lips. "The right thing?" she scoffed. "The right thing would have been to come home and be with me.

To be there when our son was born! What you did was hide. How could you think that I would resent you? I love you! I don't care if you have one leg or three heads. So long as your heart beats I am happy." She turned away from him and went to sit down on the bed. She smoothed out the skirt on her black dress and then looked up again. "I mourned you," she said sadly. "I died inside."

William didn't know what to say or feel. The only thing he knew was that the little baby in the dining room was a son. He was father to a son.

"I was in a dark place, Kitty," he breathed. "I made the decision when I'd just woken up without my leg. I was thinking that it was the end of the world. I was thinking that if I came home without a leg you would reject me and regret marrying me." He stood there awkwardly not knowing what to do. He wanted to join her on the bed but he didn't want to push her.

She leaned over to the bedside table and grabbed her black bonnet. With one swift motion she threw it at William with force. He caught the bonnet before it connected with him and peered at her curiously. "That's for thinking that I wouldn't love you if you didn't have all of your limbs." She sighed and looked at him sadly. "I understand why you did it. I understand your reasoning ... it just hurts me that you thought I would leave you because of something that happened when you performed such a heroic act. You're a hero, darling. I won't ever stop loving you, not matter what you say or do. I don't know whether that's a good thing at the moment, I'm blindly trusting you. Are you planning on leaving us again anytime soon?"

William knew hew question was completely genuine. "If you'll have me, I'll never leave you, either of you, ever again. The decision I made was that of a man who had just woken up in a hospital in a foreign country. I didn't know what to do, so I made a choice for you that was wrong. All I can do is apologise and hope you'll forgive me."

Kitty seemed to believe him. She stood up from the bed and came over to hug him once again. This time he wrapped his arms around her tightly and inhaled her sweet scent. "Every time I look at your leg I will know that my husband is the bravest man I know," she sighed into his chest.

"I hope our son with think the same way," he replied softly. "What is his name?"

"He's named for his father and mind – William Sebastian Aubrey – we call him 'Will'," Kitty said, looking up at him. That familiar look of delight had returned to her eyes again. "He has your eyes. It was as if you were looking out at me every time Will opened them."

"You named him for me?" he asked in disbelief.

"Of course," she smiled. "Don't ever break me again, I don't think my heart could take it."

William would live with that guilt for the rest of his life. But so long as he had Kitty at his side, he knew that he could handle it. "I won't," he promised. "Do you think I could meet my son before I go back to face your family?"

She nodded. "That can be arranged."

Chapter 22

Kitty watched in awe as her husband took their son in his arms for the first time. His looked at him with such love and devotion, the same feeling that she got every time she thought of Will. It was a sight she was sure she would never see. She was sure that Will would never have a father and she was sure that she would always feel empty. But that didn't have to be anymore.

The looks on both John and Kathleen's faces made it clear that they were not impressed with their son, as she was sure many people would be. But they wouldn't understand. Only she understood as only she knew his mind fully. He was trying to protect her by the only way he knew how – by being noble.

Even if it had torn her to pieces, she knew why he did it. She could see his logic in it. There would be many women who would turn their back on their husbands who came back from battle without a limb, but that wasn't her.

She had him back, and he wasn't going anywhere. She felt as if her three month long nightmare was over, and she was finally able to wake up. Losing him was the hardest thing she'd ever been through, she wouldn't wish that on anyone, not even her worst enemy.

Will stirred and opened his eyes. His bright blue irises stared at his father curiously.

"My eyes," William smiled, sounding astonished. "He looks like me."

Kathleen pursed her lips. Although she still appeared displeased, she couldn't help but smile at the sight of her son holding his child. "He does," she agreed. "How old is he exactly, Kitty?"

"He was born on the twelfth of March," Kitty replied. "So he is a month old."

William's eyes flashed to hers. "Happy birthday ... I missed it while I was ... detained."

"It was quiet," Kitty dismissed it.

William looked as if he felt as guilty as ever. She was sure that this feeling would remain for a long while, and she was positive her protective father would be sure to make it worse.

Her eyes trailed down to his left leg. It would take getting used to on her part. It didn't disgust her or frighten her, it would be a constant reminder of his bravery. But it would always be a constant reminder of the fact that he thought her capable of turning her back on him. She wouldn't ever, and he wouldn't do it to her, she wouldn't let him.

Will started to grizzle in his father's arms. William started to panic. "Does he not like me?" he fretted.

Kitty smiled. "He's hungry," she assured him.

"Did you bring your wet nurse with you, Kitty?" Kathleen asked her, looking out into the living room to see if she'd missed welcoming anyone.

"No," Kitty shook her head. She took Will from William's arms and cradled him. "I feed him myself. Mama never had one with my brothers and sisters, so I shan't have one. He is my baby, I shall be the one to feed him, not some stranger."

That night, after supper had been eaten and Will had been put to sleep in William's old, wooden cradle, Kitty and William lay in William's narrow, childhood bed.

Both of them lay on their sides watching their son sleep soundly a few feet from them.

"I am so sorry, Kitty," he whispered into her hair for the thousandth time.

"I know you are," she replied at the same decibel. She moved slightly in the bed and her bare foot brushed up against his wooden leg. He was still wearing his slacks and his thin cotton socks. She believed he was trying to hide the leg out of shame. "Why don't you take it off?" she suggested quietly.

She knew he was aware of what she was talking about as his body stiffened ever so slightly. "I'd rather not," he replied after a while.

Kitty rolled over to face him so that they were facing each other. Even in the dark, his bright blue irises were smouldering. "Why?" she pressed.

"Don't make me say it," he said in a pained voice.

"You're afraid that I'm still going to change my mind, aren't you?" she whispered in an icy tone. "You don't want me to see you without the leg."

William closed his eyes looking pained. Kitty took it as an opportunity. She threw the blankets on the bed back and got her hands on his wooden leg before he had a chance to stop her.

"Kitty, no!" he cried, reaching for her but he stopped when Will stirred. He didn't cry, but he made noises that let them no he was awake.

Kitty, rather roughly, pushed the leg of his slacks up past his knee and then pulled his sock off. It looked exactly like a leg in the way it was carved. If his skin was darker then it might have even passed for rough skin. It was attached to his leg via a leather strap around his mid – thigh. William gave up fighting her. He just looked like he had been punched in the gut.

Kitty unbuckled the strap and pulled the leg away from his body. His leg just ended at his knee. Where his leg should be was a scarred stump. The skin had healed but she could tell the wound had been nasty ... painful.

She timidly placed her hand on the scars and felt the indentations they made on his skin. She looked up to see his face and he looked more scared than ever. She knew of one thing that would convince him that she wasn't turning her back on him. She leaned down and placed a soft kiss on the bottom of his stump. "The leg does not belong in the bed, do I make myself clear?" she instructed as she looked up at him once more.

His expression had changed to one of astonishment. "You're incredible."

She smiled as she placed his leg on the floor beside the bed. "Do not ever doubt me again," she whispered, leaning into kiss him. When she pulled away from him, she sighed contently.

"What is it?"

"You can't know how hard it was for me to lose you," she said quietly. "If it had not been for Will, I don't think I could have gone on living."

William looked completely pained. He pulled her into his chest and rested his chin on top of her head. "I was trying to do the right thing," he said almost inaudibly.

Kitty touched her leg to his amputated one just to let him know that it was alright. "I know you were. I see that, but there will be a lot of people who don't see it that way."

"You father for one," he groaned quietly. "I may die for real this time."

"Papa will be angry, but if I explain he will listen to me. I will write him and mama tomorrow and let them know what's happened. That way they will be prepared for when we go home." Kitty closed her eyes and leaned against his chest. "All will be well. We can then carry on with our lives."

"I've to report to the navy when we return also. I owe Commander Gates a lot, the least I can do is elevate his military rank."

"Will you still work in the navy?" Kitty asked worriedly. She didn't want him going on any more voyages. She was certain they were not safe.

"I'm not sure," he replied honestly. "I haven't any other talents. But I am not leaving you and Will again. I will find something to do – do you want to remain living in London?"

Kitty remembered him saying something long ago about wanting to live by the sea. How it held special importance to him. "We do not have to live in London if you do not want to. I know how much you love the sea." Truthfully, she didn't want to leave London. She loved being in town and seeing familiar faces. She loved being near her family. She loved that even if her sister had married and was living apart, she was only a short carriage ride from her. She didn't like being secluded in country estates like the one her aunt and uncle lived on.

"I will always have salt water flowing through my veins," William replied. "But there are two very important people holding me to land, and I know where they want to stay."

Kitty smiled, though he couldn't see her. "Thank you," she whispered.

A week later the young family were ready to leave Kent for London. Kitty had written to her family yet she hadn't received a response, something that made William feel ill. She just assured him that they probably hadn't had an opportunity to write back. She, however, knew that wasn't the case.

Prying Will away from Kathleen's arms was a tough job. She was a very proud grandmamma and adored her little grandson.

After spending a week with his parents, their relationship seemed a little better. After a few more days of explaining what had happened and what exactly had been going through his mind when he made the decision to appear dead. Although they still didn't approve, she was sure that they understood, just as she hoped her own family would.

"You're a good girl, Lady Kitty," John smiled at his daughter – in – law as they prepared to leave. "A good wife and a good mother. You are wise beyond your years."

Kitty smiled widely at her father – in – law. "Thank you, Mr Aubrey, but I am no longer a lady, just 'Kitty'," she corrected him.

"You will always be a lady, Lady Kitty," he persisted. "Just as my son will always be a captain even if he no long returns to the navy."

Kitty gave the man a warm hug and kissed his cheek. "We shall see you for Easter, yes?" she asked as she pulled back. "Mama always makes a big spectacle. Even as adults we still paint eggs." She would strive to give her son the exact kind of childhood that she had. Her parents allowed them to do whatever they wanted ... within reason ... and they were never physically punished. Holidays were a huge deal and governesses outside of the schoolroom were never kept. It was perfect.

"Yes, we shall see you in a few weeks," he agreed. "I guarantee Kathleen will be counting down the days."

William returned from packing the carriage with the driver named Charlie that he had paid to stay in town for the week. As Kitty went over to Kathleen he began saying goodbye to his father.

"And you can come and stay with grandmamma any time you like," she cooed to Will who gurgled a response. His wide blue eyes were taking in his surroundings curiously. "And just as soon as you can stand we'll have you wading in the sea like your papa used to when he was a little boy."

Kitty laughed lightly as she heard the conversation. "I'm sure he will have salt water in his veins, just like his papa," she said, using William's words from the other week.

Kathleen leaned down and gave Will a soft kiss. "I assume you and William will be staying in London?"

Kitty nodded, feeling a little guilty. "Yes, we will," she answered sheepishly.

Kathleen seemed to accept it. "I suggest you take a house with room for us to visit from time to time. I want to have a strong relationship with my grandchildren."

"Grandchild," Kitty corrected her. "Singular."

"For now," she replied knowingly.

Kitty hoped that she would only have a single child for a while. It would take her some getting used to. But then, she realised, her mother had given birth to five children in quick succession so it was highly unlikely.

Kathleen handed her back Will and Kitty got him settled in her arms. "Thank you for your hospitality," she said gratefully. "I hope you won't be too angry with William, his heart was in the right place."

Kathleen pursed her lips and nodded. "I know it was. He's always been too noble for his own good." Kitty noticed that her eyes drifted to William's left leg. She sighed sadly. "It is such a shame. He's so young and healthy. It is not fair."

"I don't look at it like that, it is a symbol of his bravery," Kitty smiled proudly.

"Then you are a better woman than I," Kathleen replied. "Travel safely, and write to us once you've arrived. I hope you family will forgive William."

"As do I," she said nervously. She really hoped they did.

Chapter 23

With a stop overnight, they'd arrived back in London by mid – afternoon the next day. The house, to Kitty, felt quite frightening. She loved it, it was home, but she knew that once she entered the doors there was to be a lot of friction, particularly from her parents.

William took her hand comfortingly. She was alarmed that it was actually him calming her and not the other way around. "I'm prepared," he told her. "Whatever they want to say or do to me I'll accept. Your father doesn't own a musket, does he?"

Kitty shrugged her shoulders with a nervous smile. "I'm not sure, we never spent much time going through the cupboards. He won't shoot you ... I don't think."

"That's reassuring." He rolled his eyes.

Out the front of the gates was the carriage owned by her family that she had sent home when she had arrived. Considering William had already paid five pounds for Charlie's services it seemed like a waste of money to dismiss him without getting their money's worth.

Charlie helped them both down from the carriage and then proceeded to unload Kitty's trunk and William's small bag.

Kitty cuddled her son to her chest as William put his arm around her waist. Together they walked through the gates and up the stairs towards the house. Before they reached the door it was opened by Mr Carter who was looking at William with an astonished expression. "Lady Kitty," he coughed. "Captain Aubrey."

"Hello, Mr Carter," Kitty smiled kindly, trying to appear as normal as possible. She was still wearing her black mourning clothes as she brought no others with her to Kent, but if she got to opportunity she would change.

"Mr Carter," William nodded respectfully.

They walked through the doors into the foyer where her family had all assembled. Like Mr Carter they all wore the same expressions. Kitty had explained to them what had happened in her letter, detailing the fact that William had lost his leg and he was trying to save her from a life of nursing him by 'dying' in the attack. She didn't know how her family felt about it though ... they could have been murderously angry for all she knew.

Her father's eyes were the ones she caught first. He wasn't glaring per se but he was looking at William with quite a look of fury. Her mother didn't share the same look, she looked quite relieved to see him there. Her brother just looked surprised to see his brother – in – law standing there alive and Little J was beaming. Maybe she saw the noble side of the story.

"I couldn't believe it until I saw him with my own eyes," Emilia breathed, gesturing to her black dress. "It's good to have you back, William, I am so glad you're alright." She came over hurriedly and gave him a tight hug, the kind a mother would give her son. James shook his hand and Little J hugged him as well.

Sebastian remained where he stood. His arms folded across his chest and he breathed deeply.

"Lord Ethridge," William said, trying to sound confident. "You may not approve of what I did, but it was what I thought Kitty would want in the moment. I see now it was the wrong decision and I'm grateful Kitty was able to forgive me."

Sebastian arched one of his eyebrows and sneered. "You and I need to have a little conversation," he said intimidatingly. "Alone."

Kitty knew he was to be berated. "Papa, might I come with him?" she asked quietly.

"No," he said firmly.

"Sebastian," Emilia hissed. "It's very romantic."

Sebastian scoffed. "Yours and my opinions on what is romantic differ quite substantially, Em. I would never leave you voluntarily."

Kitty sighed, knowing her father didn't understand. She hoped he would give William the opportunity to explain.

Emilia only rolled her eyes before gesturing to Kitty to follow her. "Come on, darling. Papa feels the need to exercise his seniority." She shot Sebastian a very obvious annoyed look.

Kitty tried not to smile. Her mother was angry with her father and that meant he was in for a world of grovelling when they were alone. She stood on her toes and kissed William's tense jaw. He seemed to relax a little with her touch.

"Just tell him the truth. If he doesn't understand then I will speak to him."

Kitty followed her mother and siblings from the foyer into the drawing room. Little J shut the door behind him so William and Sebastian could go off to the office. Emilia took her grandson from Kitty's arms.

Tea and finger sandwiches were already in the room. Kitty was grateful, she was quite hungry from the journey.

"Must I be with the women, mama?" James complained. "This is such a feminine house."

"Would you rather be with Miss Snooty Smith?" Little J giggled as the four of them and baby Will sat down on the opposing settees.

"Stop calling her that!" James groaned. "She's not snooty."

"Yes, she is," Emilia agreed. Kitty's eyes widened at her mother's brazen comment.

"Mama," James rolled his eyes. "She's just rich."

"So are we," Little J shot back. "And we're not snooty."

Miss Sarah Smith was an ongoing presence in her brother's life. She hoped he wouldn't make an offer for her, she didn't want to have to see her at family gatherings. Seeing her at social gatherings was enough. She was pretty, very voluptuous. She was sure her brother's interest stemmed from there.

"Her father is wealthy, there is a difference," Emilia interjected. "She has two elder brothers. Without an advantageous marriage she will be nothing, and you, my dear son, are an advantageous marriage. Show me a woman who hates your title and you have my blessing."

James picked up a couple of finger sandwiches and began to eat them. "I'm not planning on proposing anytime soon," he assured them. "I'm still young. Marriage is for when you're old."

Kitty scoffed in mock horror. "We are twins, James. I am married!"

"For five minutes," he muttered.

"For ten months and counting. He was never dead, he was alive the whole time," Kitty retorted.

"I thought what William did was very noble. Not only did he save a lesser officer's life, he didn't want to burden you with the result," Little J said approvingly.

"As I said, I thought it was romantic," her mother agreed. "How did you find out he was alive?" Emilia asked and smiled as Will curled his tiny fingers around hers. Kitty loved it when he did that.

"He was with his parents when I arrived. He was to stop there and return to London permanently after. He has to report to the navy, he's planning on making sure Commander Gates' rank is elevated," Kitty explained.

"What's his fake leg like?" James asked curiously. Kitty shot an annoyed look to her brother. His dark blue eyes were wide with inquisitiveness.

Kitty made a face. Only her brother would insist on making a point of the existence of his false leg. "It is exquisitely made," she answered simply. "Jamaican carpenters are the very best, in my opinion."

"It doesn't make you squeamish ... because you are a bit of a girl, Kitty," James grinned childishly.

"Oh, well spotted," she quipped sarcastically. "No, it doesn't make me squeamish. It shows me and everyone that knows that he is an incredibly brave man. He endured such pain to save someone who was of a lesser rank than him."

"Amputation is truly marvellous if you ask me," Little J chimed in. "For hundreds of years lives have been saved by simply removing a limb. Years ago people just died from their wounds because they didn't know that someone could live without an arm or a leg. And nowadays the false legs can be crafted to look just like real legs. It's absolutely fascinating."

Kitty, Emilia and James all stared at Little J.

She pursed her lips self – consciously. "Or so I've heard. What? I read a lot!"

Emilia laughed lightly. "Don't worry, dear, the facts that you inform us with teach us all so much."

"Thank you, mama," Little J sighed, sounding disheartened. "It is because I'm female that I sound ridiculous? Nobody would ever rely on me because of my sex, could they?"

Kitty hated how her younger sister felt ridiculed because of her intelligence. She hated how society damned women to kitchens and nursery's whilst men were allowed to do whatever they wanted. One day she would like to vote on who would be prime minister – but that would never happen. They lived in a man's world.

"Little J, how could you say such things?" Emilia gasped. "You know we've always encouraged your mind. You are so bright, Little J!"

"Don't ever let anybody make you feel as though you aren't worthy of what you want, Little J. If they do then you will report them directly to me," James spoke defensively.

Little J looked at her brother gratefully. Kitty was surprised at the sudden show of affection that her brother displayed. There weren't many men that would defend a woman with cleverness in her acquaintance, but she was glad her brother was one of them.

"Now why can't you behave as wisely when it comes to Snooty Smith?" her mother said exasperatedly.

Kitty giggled as James rolled his eyes. She was sure the Sarah Smith debacle would sort itself out in due course.

William was sweating bullets as Sebastian led him into his study. The Earl was wearing a black mourning coat with matching black slacks and boots. It made him feel exceptionally guilty thinking how many people had gone into mourning for him.

Sebastian took a seat in the big leather chair behind the large, mahogany desk which left the smaller chairs before the desk for him. He chose the one on the left and sat down silently.

Sebastian's dark blue eyes bore into him. It was alarming how they mirrored Kitty's yet the looks that came out of them were completely different. Sebastian took a deep breath and seemed to wait for William to begin.

"I know I must apologise to you, Lord Ethridge. When I made the decision I did not imagine the repercussions. I now know it was a foolish decision," he began sincerely.

"It was," he answered sternly. He did not give anything away, it was as if he wanted William to beg for his forgiveness.

"I know I hurt Kitty with my decision, but at the time I truly thought it best," he continued. "It was before a leg was made for me, before I knew I would be able to walk with some normality. If I'd have known all these things back then the letter would have never been sent. But you've got to understand, I woke up with a piece of me missing. My leg was gone. Some doctor had hacked it off when I had been unconscious. I was in shock ... I wasn't thinking clearly."

Sebastian's eyes narrowed. "Obviously."

William sighed. "Kitty has forgiven me, is that not enough for you? I know you are a nobleman and I'm just a military man but I don't know what you want me to say."

"Kitty was gone," he retorted immediately. "My exasperatingly lively daughter was gone. She didn't eat or sleep. She just lay on her bed staring out of the window."

William felt immediately guilty for his snide comment. This man was only looking out for his daughter the same way he would always look out for his son. It was a paternal thing. "It was a mistake, one I will pay for, for the rest of my life. I missed my son's birth."

"Raising her, it was a triumph if we could get her to sit still for more than ten minutes. They went through about seven governesses in the blink of an eye. She's ... one of a kind. Like any of my children, I won't see any of them hurt."

William knew very well how unique Kitty was. She accepted a husband with a false leg. She was incredible. "I won't hurt her, not again. I won't ever leave her. I won't ever leave them both. I love them, more than anything."

"I don't care if I hang. If you hurt my little girl again I will kill you in the slowest and most painful way I possibly can. I'll scrape your innards out with a spoon." Sebastian's serious glare never faltered so William knew he was completely serious.

"I understand, sir," he replied formally.

Sebastian smiled slightly before his serious look returned. "How are you adjusting?" he asked, nodding toward his leg.

"Slowly but surely. I'm not a fast walker, I won't ever run, but I can move. It is better than being bedridden. I have it better than a lot of people." He was getting used to the leg. He hoped sooner rather then later he would have a somewhat normal walking pattern.

"Are you to remain in the navy?"

"I don't know. I'm going to go and speak to my superiors tomorrow. I need to give a report on the loyalty of my men as well as a full account of what happened. I want to get Commander Gates a higher rank. As for me, well, I don't know what they'll want to do with me. I don't want to ever go out on a voyage again. My priorities lie here."

Sebastian seemed satisfied with his answer. "Good," he approved. "If the navy does not want you, then I'm sure there is something around here we could have you do. Are you any good with management?"

"As in monetary management?" William checked.

"I do the managing of my estate myself. You should have seen the state of it when I inherited. I've completely turning it around. But it would be nice not to have to worry about doing it all myself. It's just something to think about, you are my son – in – law, after all." Sebastian rose from his chair and walked around to the other side of the desk. "But something tells me you are not the type of man who enjoys sitting behind a desk and writing papers all day."

William shook his head. "To be honest, no. The navy held a purpose for me."

"Then I'm sure they will have something for you to do," he concluded. "A decorated captain, such as yourself, will not be discarded. Now come along. No doubt the family thinks I've murdered you. I've got to go and grovel to my wife. She thinks what you did for Kitty was outrageously romantic."

William smiled a small smile. He knew Sebastian was still cautious – any good father would be – but he thought he understood. He also believed Sebastian trusted him not to hurt Kitty again. He didn't doubt the Earl's threat to gut him with a spoon if he did.

Chapter 24

Leaving Will in the care of Emilia and Sebastian, Kitty and William ventured into the London naval base to allow William to give his report on what happened to the Admiral of the Fleet – Martin Gregson. The meeting had been arranged some weeks ago and Kitty was quite excited to be meeting William's superiors.

William wasn't as excited. Kitty knew he was nervous about the outcome. The navy was aware of his original plan to 'fake' his death, and they knew of his amputation. They knew everything and they were well within their rights to dismiss him and strip of him of his decorations. He hoped that he would be able to retire honourably. Any other way would just have been humiliating for him.

The base was not what Kitty expected. She expected the building to be less impressive. It was quite a rustic looking structure. The columns that supported the upper level were made of beautiful sandstone and the shutters and frames were all a brilliant royal blue. There were two flags being flown – one was the flag of England and the other was the flag of Great Britain.

Kitty took her husband's hand as they exited the carriage. She gave him a reassuring smile and nodded with encouragement. As they walked through the doors Kitty herself felt a panic consume her. She felt completely underdressed. She was wearing a simple cream coloured dress with a pale green ribbon tied around her waist. There was nothing incredibly special about her dress which made her feel inferior when looking at the luxurious furnishings of the King's naval base.

William was wearing his naval uniform with all his decorations, in particular his gold hilted sword. His posture was completely rigid and his dark blond hair was neatly combed back.

Two men came out of the double doors to the left of him. She had no idea whether they were of a higher rank to William or not but nevertheless they both saluted her husband and he them.

"Admiral Gregson will see you now, Captain," the first man said. He looked young, younger than Kitty even so he had to be of a lesser rank.

"Thank you, Lieutenant," William replied stiffly.

Both men looked at Kitty curiously which made her question her right to be there. Perhaps she was to wait outside. But William took her with him anyway, not giving her the opportunity to remain behind.

The Admiral of the Fleet's office looked remarkably similar to her own father's office. The walls were lined with mahogany bookshelves filled with all sort of titles and genres. The centre of the room was dominated with a large oak desk neatly organised. The floor was blood red carpet and felt soft underneath her feet. The most remarkable thing in the room, however, was the man sitting behind the desk.

It was clear that he was in charge. He gave off an air of superiority, one that trumped William's when she first met him. His green eyes were wise and somewhat calm. His dark hair was greying and he looked to be a little older that her father. His naval uniform was covered in medals and decorations to show off his many accomplishments that led him to the top job.

William saluted his commanding officer formally and Admiral Gregson returned the gesture. Kitty didn't know what to do. Clearly she shouldn't salute so instead she curtseyed slightly, feeling like an imbecile.

"Captain, milady, take a seat," he said, sounding quite docile, as he gestured to the wooden chairs before him.

Kitty tried to hide her nervous jitters as she sat down in the chair before the most important man in the navy. He sat down in the grand chair behind the desk and looked at the both of them.

"I've never really liked this office," he said, somewhat casually. "It's nothing like the feeling of being at the helm."

"I know exactly how you feel, sir," William replied, smiling slightly.

"We're all men, Captain … bar your lovely wife, of course," he said, nodding to Kitty. "We've all made decisions that we're not proud of and we all bear scars that burden us. I, myself, do as well." Admiral Gregson held up his left hand that had been previously concealed at his side. His ring and little fingers were missing, the remains were quite badly burned.

An unorthodox gasp escaped Kitty's lips. "I beg your pardon," she asked immediately after.

Admiral Gregson chuckled lightly. "It's quite alright, milady. It happened twenty years ago when I was just a cadet. I loaded a cannon incorrectly and boom. I was lucky my whole hand wasn't blown off." Kitty was amazed that he referred to such a horrendous accident so casually. "But what I'm saying is, and I will have your epaulettes if this ever gets back to my wife, that men often make brash choices when faced with difficult situations."

"I don't understand, sir, am I to receive a punishment?" William asked slowly. "I was fully expecting to turn in my epaulettes today."

Admiral Gregson furrowed his brows. "The navy does not care what you and your wife do, Captain, we care about your actions while you are serving in His Majesty's name. You did everything right, Captain Aubrey. You were faced with a surprise attack and you handled it correctly. You assembled your crew and loaded the guns. You protected your charge and the cargo was safely delivered without harm. Although three men did lose their lives, it could have been much worse had you not acted as quickly as you did. I'm also told that the amputation of your leg was a result of a heroic act to save Commander George Gates' life, is that correct?"

William looked uncomfortable as the Admiral of the Fleet praised him.

Kitty decided to interject, whether it was her place or not. "That is true, sir," she nodded. "The mast had been severed and had William .... Captain Aubrey ... not pushed him out of the way he surely would have been killed."

"Your wife seems very proud of you, Captain," Admiral Gregson noted.

William's bright blue eyes shone as he looked to Kitty quickly. "I don't deserve her," he replied simply. "I may have lost my leg and my career but I still have her and our son."

"A child? Oh, many congratulations," Admiral Gregson beamed. "But you still do not understand why I have called you here, do you, Captain? You are not losing your career. Your epaulettes will be removed and replaced with new ones."

William frowned questioningly. "New ones, sir?"

At that moment the doors to the office opened abruptly and Admiral Gregson immediately stood. Kitty and William stood as well and turned around to see who the interrupter was.

His hair was white and his clothes were very fine ... regally fine in fact. His suit was made from green velvet and his cloak was decorated with what looked like a solid gold chain. Kitty knew exactly who their distinguished intruder was. She, William and Admiral Gregson came out from behind the chairs and the desk.

Kitty curtseyed deeply and both William and Admiral Gregson bowed with respect.

"Your Majesty, you are right on time," Admiral Gregson smiled at his King.

King William IV nodded in agreement. "Of course, I was not going to be late to meed a patriot."

William looked shocked. Kitty was just as surprised. She was in the room with the Sovereign. He was the King of the British Empire. She was meeting the King!

"Your Majesty, allow me to introduce Captain William Aubrey, and his wife Lady Catherine Aubrey," Admiral Gregson said.

Kitty did not want to King to know her more informal and somewhat inappropriate nickname. Even if she did not like her first name, she would not be known as 'Kitty' to the King.

"Absolute pleasure," King William nodded to both William and Kitty. "I am informed of every endeavour undertaken by our military units and I was humbled to know that there are still men like you in the navy, Captain."

"Thank you, Your Majesty," William managed to choke out. Kitty was still in complete and utter shock.

The King looked at him proudly. "It is men like you that make the navy what it is. You are being given the title of Commodore."

"Commodore?" William coughed. "Me?"

"You are free to refuse, of course," the King said casually.

"No, Your Majesty," William said quickly. "I just had no idea that I would be receiving a promotion when I cam here today."

"You are a distinguished and decorated officer, Commodore Aubrey. I am surprised at your astonishment," the King commented.

Kitty could not believe that they were conversing with the King. Her family would never believe it.

"It is a shame you're married, Commodore Aubrey," the King continued. "For I would have liked to introduce you to my niece, Princess Victoria. She's a lovely young thing. She is fourteen, but in a few years would have been perfect for you."

William relaxed a little at the casual comment. "I thank you, Your Majesty. I'm sure Princess Victoria is lovely, but I think we can both agree that there are none that can equal my wife." He took Kitty's hand in his and squeezed it tight.

Kitty could not believe he husband had just dismissed a Princess. Was that not an insult? He would have never been able to marry a Princess anyway, he wasn't royalty.

Instead the King chuckled. "I agree, she is very fair," he nodded.

Her eyes widened. "Thank you," she managed quietly. The King had just called her 'fair'.

"But I fear I cannot take all the credit, Commander George Gates showed more loyalty and courage than any other offi-cer I have ever had the pleasure to sail with. He in the unsung hero of that attack," William said proudly, as if he was talking of his protégé.

"Yes, I'm aware of him. You may as well pass on your epaulettes to him, Commodore," Admiral Gregson comment-ed. "He will be given the rank of Captain."

William smiled proudly. "Thank you, sir," he said to Admiral Gregson. "He will not disappoint you."

"I heard you lost your leg as well, Commodore," the King said, returning the attention back to him.

Both Kitty and William looked down to William's concealed false leg. "Yes, I did," he replied, sounding less enthused.

"I am sorry," the King apologised.

"It is alright."

"What would you like to do, Commodore? We have seas and land naval positions for you. With a young child ... perhaps you would like to reside here in London?" Admiral Gregson suggested.

Kitty nodded without thinking. Both the King and Admiral Gregson laughed.

"Yes, sir," William replied, squeezing Kitty's hand again.

"Well then, you will be in charge of all cadet training, Commodore. You will also be in charge of the ships that dock here in London. Does that sound like something you can do, Commodore?" Admiral Gregson proposed.

William smiled widely. "Yes, sir, it does. I will not let you down."

"You won't," the King said surely. "I take an interest in particular military men, Commodore Aubrey, you are one of them. I will take my leave now."

They all bowed and curtseyed once more as the King departed the room.

"Congratulations, Commodore," Admiral Gregson commended. "When would you like to commence work?"

"As soon as possible," William replied.

"Well then, we shall see you at the beginning of next week. The position comes with a house and staff as well as a carriage. You will be quite comfortable there ... plenty of room for familial additions," he hinted.

Kitty felt her cheeks redden at the comment. She wanted plenty of familial additions, but discussing them with the Admiral of the Fleet was a little embarrassing.

"I am really grateful, sir," William said sincerely. "I had thought for sure I would never serve the navy ever again."

"An injury, regardless of how serious, does not warrant dismissal, Commodore. Thank me by serving your country for the remainder of your days." Admiral Gregson saluted William and he reciprocated.

They departed arm in arm and William wore the biggest grin on his face. Kitty could not have been more proud of him. He was the best man she had ever known. She knew he would do anything for her, even giving up his career, but he didn't have to do that. He could have the best of both worlds and so could she.

Everything was falling into place, and she didn't feel like it was too good to be true this time.

Epilogue

Kitty caressed her rounded stomach as summer came to an end. She hadn't participated in the seasonal activities as much, instead choosing to spend time with her family.

Annie had given birth to a girl, little Amy. She and Joseph were elated and a large christening had been held for her at her father's expense, not that he minded. Amy was a very pretty, docile baby. She'd inherited her mother's brown eyes and light blonde hair. Everyone was convinced she would be the talk of the town in eighteen years.

James was still courting Miss Sarah Smith and had assured his family that any talk of an engagement was far away.

Henry had graduated from Eton in June and was now enrolled at Cambridge studying law much to their parent's delight.

And Little J. Little J was still sneaking off as usual. She had turned one and twenty and their parents were now wanting her to get more invested in finding a husband. They didn't mind if he wasn't noble, and they didn't mind if she waited a few more years, but she didn't show any interest in marrying any of the men that the Alcott's socialised with.

Evangeline had married her baronet and had moved to Cheshire to his estate. They corresponded weekly. Evangeline was enjoying married life and running her own household. She wasn't with child yet, but it was only a matter of time.

But Kitty was with child once again. Will was six months old and Kitty was four months along with her and William's second child. William was really enjoying his work as Commodore at London's naval base. Every so often he would go on short journeys around Europe but he never went across to America at Kitty's insistence.

The house that they had taken was very nice. It was much smaller than Ethridge with fewer rooms, but it was still a fine place for a young family to live. They had a staff of ten. A cook, two kitchen maids, two footmen, a butler and four housemaids.

Kitty was very happy with how her life was turning out. Just over a year ago she was starting her London season as a silly young girl. Now she was leaving it as a mature mother of one, nearly two.

She sat in her parent's drawing room, bouncing her very aware son on her lap. They were having Sunday lunch after the church service. Since everyone permanently resided in London, Emilia insisted on everyone gathering on a Sunday to keep family bonds tight. Kitty enjoyed it. She loved being around her family.

"There you are," William said, entering the drawing room and closing the door behind him. "Lunch is served."

Kitty nodded and cooed to Will. "You're going to go and play with a maid for awhile so mama and papa can have some food, yes, you are!" she said in a baby voice. Will giggled and clapped his hands. He didn't know what Kitty had said but he enjoyed the interaction.

William laughed. "You sound so adorable when you speak like that."

Kitty stood up and grinned. "Why, thank you, Commodore," she said curtseying comically.

William wrapped his arm around her waist and kissed her temple. "You don't have to call me that all the time, it has been awhile since I was given the title."

"I know," she shrugged, fixing Will on her hip. "It will just be last time I'll ever get to call you that as I'll have to refer to you as 'Rear Admiral' from tomorrow onwards."

William rolled his eyes. "We don't know that's going to happen! It was only implied," he sighed.

"Implied quite obviously," Kitty smiled. "You know it's going to happen. You are very good at your job."

"Yes," he agreed. "I'm being promoted to Rear Admiral tomorrow," he said excitedly. He took Will from Kitty's arms and kissed him lightly. "Your papa's going to be a Rear Admiral!"

"I'm very proud of you," Kitty said sincerely. William turned his attention back to his wife. Whenever his bright blue eyes looked at her she could see right into them. It was as if she could read his every thought. With the way he looked at her, it was only good reading.

"I couldn't have done anything without you," he replied simply.

"True," she laughed lightly. Just as he was about to press his lips to hers the door to the drawing room opened abruptly.

A troubled looking Little J entered without knocking or announcing herself. "Oh, good, you're in here," she beamed, looking a little relieved. "William, get out."

"Little J," Kitty scolded. "That's quite rude."

Little J didn't reply. She only looked at William as if she still expected him to leave.

William chuckled at her sister's antics and kissed his wife on the cheek. "We'll be in the dining room when you're ready," he informed them both.

Once the door was closed, Little J grabbed Kitty's hand and dragged her to the settees to sit down. Kitty had absolutely no idea what had got her so riled up.

"Little J, whatever is the matter with you?" she asked, concerned.

"It's time," Little J said nervously. She brushed her loose blonde curls away from her face and knotted her hands together on the lap of her pale blue gown. Her blue eyes were questioning.

Kitty furrowed her brows. "Time for what?"

"I need your advice, Kitty. You're my sister and you're the only one I can come to about this," she stammered. "Going to Annie would just be awkward as I don't want to know about her and Reverend Joseph!"

"Little J, what is it?" Kitty pressed. She was worried, her sister never fretted like this.

"I'm in love," she groaned. She threw her head back on the settee in shame.

Kitty gasped. "Is he who you've been sneaking off to see?" She could see it now. Her sister would be ruined and thrown out of London. She would be like William's birth mother, laughed out of London with her baby taken away from her. She would die in a French convent! "Little J, please tell me you have not fallen!"

Little J shook her head. "I told you I haven't. He doesn't even know I exist. He's just a coincidence of where I've been sneaking off to. He's there every day ... he brown eyes torture me."

Kitty was shocked. Her sister truly was in love. But how could he not notice her? Perhaps he was a blind man, literally. "Are you going to tell me where you've been going?" She thought she ought to try and get it out of her. This had been the most open she'd been in months!

Little J bit her lip, toying with the decision of whether or not to tell Kitty. "Just tell me what to do first," Little J pressed. "Do I tell him how I feel? Because the yearning is eating me up inside!"

"No, you don't tell him how you feel, that's very unladylike," Kitty scolded. "Imagine what mama would say."

"Mama would probably lock me in my bedchamber if she knew and never let me out," Little J mumbled.

"Little J, if he hasn't noticed you by now then he probably won't notice you. In my opinion he's an idiot," she said simply. It was true. She had been sneaking off for a long time, if this man had been around all this time and he hadn't made a move then he probably wasn't going to.

Little J pouted. "Why must love be so hard?" she whined.

"I know, love is difficult. Men are difficult," she concurred.

Little J scoffed. "You seem to have a handle on things," she commented sarcastically.

"Not at first … second, or even third. It's taken me a long time to get where I am, Little J. I had to jump through several hoops to be as happy as I am," she said simply. Her happiness had taken quite a few turns. But she had finally come to the finish line and she could not be happier.

Little J bit her lip and thought for a moment. She sighed and began. "Okay, so you're going to think I'm crazy, and … I think it's illegal, I'm not sure. But you're my sister and I trust you. I've been going –" she started but the door to the drawing room opened once more.

"Girls?" their mother's head popped her head in the drawing room. "You are in here. I've just received a wedding invitation," she smiled.

Kitty wanted to scream. Her mother had the worst timing! Little J had just been about to tell her what she had been doing! "One minute, mama, Little J and I just need to finish discussing something." But she could tell that Little J had already changed her mind.

"Never mind," she said to her. "Who's the wedding invitation from, mama?" she asked.

"Is there something I should know?" Emilia furrowed her eyebrows, entering the room holding the ivory coloured invitation.

"No, mama," both girls said in unison.

She could tell Emilia didn't believe them but their good mama decided not to press the issue. "Come along then, it's lunchtime. And I think we all will want to discuss this invitation. It's quite a surprise … well, not really, but I think we'll all be amused."

Kitty was helped up from the settee by Little J who looped her arm through hers. Kitty had a feeling she knew who the invitation was from, and it was true, it was amusing.

As they walked through to the dining room, the sight she saw just filled her heart with warmth. William had not given baby Will to a maid, instead opting to have him up at the table on his lap. While other men shied away from their children, or showing any ounce of vulnerability, her husband didn't. She didn't mind that she'd had to jump through hoops to get this. She would do it a thousand times over just to experience the kind of love she felt for her family. She placed a soft hand on her pregnant stomach and knew that it could only get better.